GWASANAETH LLYS

I've travelled the world twice over,
Met the famous: saints and sinners,
Poets and artists, kings and queens,
Old stars and hopeful beginners,
I've been where no-one's been before,
Learned secrets from writers and cooks
All with one library ticket
To the wonderful world of books.

© JANICE JAMES.

ZODIAC

The twelve signs of the Zodiac hold fascination for everyone, since we were all born 'under' one of them. Their ancient wisdom and traditions reach back to the beginning of time, and in this book astrologer Richard Lawler conducts us on a tour of the Zodiac, its mysteries and secrets. Dilys Gater — herself a clairvoyant — has provided twelve short stories to illustrate and sum up the nature of each sign. The result opens up the mysteries of the stars and planets — as well as the quirks of the human beings who are ruled by them.

Books by Dilys Gater
Published by The House of Ulverscroft:

PREJUDICED WITNESS
THE DEVIL'S OWN
SOPHY
A BOOK CASE: A POPULAR AUTHOR'S
SUCCESS STORY
THE DARK STAR
THE LURE OF THE FALCON
THE YEAR'S AT THE SPRING
THE EMILY EXPERIMENT
PROPHECY FOR A QUEEN
A PLACE OF SAFETY
THE WITCH-GIRL

ZODIAC

Stories by Dilys Gater,
selected by Richard Lawler,
with astrological commentary.

Complete and Unabridged

ULVERSCROFT
Leicester

First Large Print Edition
published 1996

British Library CIP Data

Gater, Dilys
    Zodiac.—Large print ed.—
    Ulverscroft large print series: general fiction
    1. English fiction—20th century
    2. Large type books
    I. Title II. Lawler, Richard
    823.9'14 [F]

    ISBN 0–7089–3646–6

Published by
F. A. Thorpe (Publishing) Ltd.
Anstey, Leicestershire
Set by Words & Graphics Ltd.
Anstey, Leicestershire
Printed and bound in Great Britain by
T. J. Press (Padstow) Ltd., Padstow, Cornwall

This book is printed on acid-free paper

To our brothers and sisters
in the stars

Acknowledgements

The stories by Dilys Gater have previously appeared as follows:

Exile: Deesider Magazine.

Season Of Giving: Shropshire Magazine.

Shadow Play: The Ebb Tide and other stories from Cornwall (Weaver Press).

A Question Of Paternity: Writers News Short Story Course Handbook.

It's an Ill Wind: Dilys Gater on Short Story Writing (cassette).

A Circle Of Fear: West Wickham, Shirley and Hayes Weekly Review.

Tea For Two: BBC Merseyside.

Contents

The Authors, By Each Other

Which Sign Are You?

If you are born in a leap year most signs will start a calendar day early and finish a calendar day early.

For those born exactly on the cusps it is good to consult an astrologer, calculate on a computer or look up in an astrological table called an ephemeris for your birth year, month, day number and time.

Your place of birth may also affect these time zones. Australasia being east time is subtracted. America being west time is added. The guides given are for Greenwich mean time in London, England in the United Kingdom.

If in doubt read for both signs. Your moon, rising signs and other planets will give you mixed traits as well.

R.L.

Introduction

The World Of the Zodiac
by Richard Lawler

ASTROLOGY is the study of the stars in order to interpret the events of the Past and be able to foretell the events that are likely to happen in the future. Everyone born into the world is born, according to the lore of astrology, beneath a special star sign — their birth sign. There are twelve of these signs, which cover the period of one year, and which make up the twelve signs of the Zodiac.

Each sign of the Zodiac is made up of many parts — sun sign, influence of the moon and where the other stars and planets happen to be at any given moment. This explains why an astrological chart drawn up for one person may be anything but simple; in fact it might run into many pages. Many people deride astrology, claiming that

1

their personality bears no resemblance to their particular sun sign. But the moon represents the inner core of our nature, our emotions and spontaneous reactions.

While the sun is connected with the conscious mind which concerns itself with survival and acceptability, the moon accounts for the feelings we would sometimes prefer to ignore. It often indicates the obstacles to happiness which we sometimes create for ourselves.

The ancient Celts measured time by the moon and the night, rather than by the sun and the day. They based their calendar on the lunation cycle. Nowadays our calendar year is based on the sun while the month is roughly based on the moon's cycle.

Our star signs are constantly fluctuating. For instance, the moon changes signs approximately every two and a half days. This may account for the fact that when the moon is in Pisces you feel dreamy and sensitive, while a Virgo moon will make you efficient and organised, and if you have the moon in Taurus you are least likely to have emotional problems.

Each of the stories in this book was chosen to illustrate one particular sign of the Zodiac. Some of the illustrations are more obvious, summing up the typical qualities associated with that sign. In other cases, I wanted to illustrate less familiar qualities, or even show how the negative aspects — the reverse side of the sign, as it were — can make their appearance, and what happens then. Browsing through a selection of Dilys Gater's stories has been a pleasure rather than a duty, and I came across many characters who were immediately recognisable as highly representative of the Zodiacal sign of their birth.

In this selection, I will introduce each sign of the Zodiac and explain something about it. My choice of story to represent this sign will follow. I hope you will enjoy this celestial 'cocktail' as much as I have enjoyed putting the ingredients together.

Aries
(March 21 – April 20)

THE Sun in Aries represents a Positive, Cardinal Fire sign. This is the first sign of the Zodiac, and Arians are often self-concerned with a need to be noticed — though they are not necessarily always novel!

Strongly-held feelings promote a self-assertive way and a desire to lead for its own sake, regardless of any qualifications for doing so.

Arians are energetic, impatient, impulsive: their rashness can occasionally lead to conflict. A headstrong attitude can predominate, often resulting from insufficient prior thoughtfulness. But Arians have much cerebral power and the capacity for great intellectual activity — indeed, Aries is the 'brain-box' of the Zodiac.

Intellectually — and physically — Arians are frequently enterprising and bold: 'who dares wins' should often be their motto. Challenges are seen as opportunities and

5

stepping stones to victory.

Home life is of prime importance, the domestic environment providing spiritual replenishment. Family ties are adhered to and respected. Great awareness of personal roots, of where one is 'coming from'.

Aries is represented by the flower of the daffodil — Arians possess the almost mystical intuition and simplistic qualities of childhood, and have an innate affinity with nature. This simplistic quality means that Arians invariably aim for the heart of things in their perceptions and their actions and are able to cut through irrelevances.

They will always strive to lead; they can be stoical and will always seek independence, even if through rebellion and crusading. They can grasp essentials easily, but sometimes any inspiration received can give way to reckless, assertive, impulsive aggression.

Arians can be straightforward to the point of naïvety, but when in a moderate, tolerant and patient mood they are capable of offering a sporting chance to adversaries. Arians have a tendency to act without thinking, which may make them appear arrogant to others.

★ ★ ★

The story I have chosen as an illustration of Aries is called EXILE. This wonderfully illustrates the wilfulness of the Arian character and the arrogance of the typical Arian, together with a compensating belief that if only one tries hard enough and wants it enough, the magic will work and a miracle will happen. So often, for Arians, it does, as they are still in touch with the magic and the miracles and their personal strength can be phenomenal.

Our bossy heroine's bark is far worse than her bite. She would like us to believe she is completely in control, yet the forces which come to her aid bring out the best in her basically generous nature and help us to feel she has earned her little miracle.

Exile

It had sounded such a good idea a couple of months back when Jon propounded it to me at the tag-end of a dusty London summer, the window of his office pushed open as wide as the wretched thing would go to try and bring a breath of air into the box-like room that was almost blue with Freddie's chain-smoking.

The city still breathed the heat of the day from every gloomy brick wall that comprised our view from what we euphemistically called 'The Room at the Top'. Jon, you'll have already gathered, is a romantic at heart, and I fiercely fostered his hopes of some day making it big. He deserved to, but what mattered even more to me was that I loved him body and soul. I'd have given anything to see him get on — except listen to propositions from some of the weirdies who turned up at the modelling studio where I worked, and who indicated that they could do a lot for a struggling young photographer — at a price. If I wanted to pay that price, Jon would be made overnight, but that wouldn't have brought either of us happiness, and even I, the eternal cynic, knew it.

"*The City of Chester*," Freddie was intoning from some guide book, the day they told me about the idea, "*is haunted by the ghosts of the Roman legionnaires who were garrisoned here, who patrolled the walls of what was then Deva, outpost of the great empire that proved the truth of the saying that all roads led to Rome — .*"

"See what I'm getting at?" Jon turned to me. "We set it all up — the centurion standing on those Roman walls, a lone figure far from his home staring out across the wilds of exile — I can link it up with some of the pix we've got on file of the refugees — you know the ones I mean — ."

"It's great," I said, but I'd have said that even if it hadn't been. For the smile, the enthusiasm in his dark blue eyes, I'd have said anything. But it really was great.

Only now that we were standing on these same Roman walls, and they were dim with a veil of drifting snowflakes, and there was a sort of grey fog everywhere that made the city look like a pencil drawing somebody had smudged, the cynic in me was having a few second thoughts. In spite of the fact that I was buried in my fake fur coat so that only my nose was visible, it was darned cold, and the romance of the exile far from his home was rapidly becoming less romantic. I wondered vaguely, as I watched Freddie and Jon clatter up some steps that led to a sort of bridge that crossed a main road (they called them Gates here in Chester) why we couldn't have had an exile in Hawaii or even Napoleon on Elba — anywhere where there was some sun.

Our centurion, a burly actor called — with painful whimsy — Smith Smith ('that way, no management ever forgets my name') turned round to leer at me. He'd been doing that on and off ever since we were introduced, but I was adept at withering looks by now. You caught on fast at the studio.

"After you, madame," he said, indicating the steps with loaded gallantry that cut no ice with me. I didn't want those wandering hands of his 'helping me up' by pawing at what he could find of my legs if I preceded him into the crummy little tower that stood at the top of the steps.

"You go," I said shortly. "I expect

they're setting up further along, they'll want you. I'll hang around for a few minutes."

"Don't get yourself lost, darling," he murmured in his best deep brown velvet voice.

"You've got to be kidding," I said. "These walls only go one way, right round in a circle. I'll meet you all coming back."

But I didn't move, even after he had gone. It was unbelievably melancholy there in the grey mist that hid the ruins of that ancient Roman city beneath the concrete and the clay. I leaned my fake-fur clad arms on the wall. I might have been alone in the world. It was so still, in spite of the lights winking through all the colours of Christmas, the muted babble of crowds somewhere in the far distance, fighting each other in the commercial rush. Don't get yourself lost, darling, the very words false, fake, sham. It came to me then that I was already lost, that somehow I'd strayed a long way from everything that had been so right, so natural, in the old days. Values. Goodness. Truth.

11

Oh my God, I thought, don't start that! What does it matter? So things didn't work out the way you expected they would? You dreamed romantic dreams of tall dark strangers, flowers and orange blossom, stars and violins, true love and happy ever after, amen? So you're stuck with working in a place you hate, selling yourself to the eyes of gawping cameras, because that's what brings in the money and there's a living to be earned? You got the true love in the end, didn't you? That's more than most girls get in a lifetime, you got Jon.

It didn't take the sudden dark mood away, though, this time. Everything was so wrong, so wrong. Jon was honest and true as bread, trying to persuade a world that didn't want to know, that his work was good; trying to follow his own heart's dictates when the judgements that were passed on everything he did were coloured by the falsity of commercialism. He wouldn't stoop to anything dishonourable, he wouldn't lie or crawl or toady to anybody. He had so much to give — so very much — and nobody wanted to take it, nobody wanted to see that truth shining through. There must be somebody — somewhere — I thought, overcome by such hopelessness and despair that tears of helpless rage started to my eyes, and I banged my clenched fist against the wall through my glove, wishing with all my heart that I could make people see.

A long time later, I turned, the cynical mask snapping back. Two figures were looming out of the mist, battling their way against the clinging snowflakes with the determined doggedness of true Britishers. Heavily clad in unisex macintoshes, laden like pack-horses with bags full of what I deduced to be Christmas shopping. As a final touch, a small spiky evergreen tree, strapped to a pair of staunch, though elderly shoulders, stuck up like a flagpole.

Mr Everyman and his wife, judging by the conservative bristle-brush moustache and the few grey curls that were visible beneath a luridly patterned head-scarf. They passed me with the half-shy averting of the eyes by means of which complete strangers acknowledge each other's presence, and prepared to mount the steps to the tower, or turret or whatever it was. Then they must have suffered what was probably the shock of their staid and solid lives.

A voice splintered the frosty air, boomed into the grey mist.

"*Salvete! Miles Romanus sum. Qui estis?? Quo vaditis? Dicete!*"

Huh, I thought sarcastically. The burly figure of Smith Smith might wow them in the aisles in a juvenile production of *Julius Caesar*, but would hardly make managements reach for their gold-topped pens and start signing contracts. Mr Everyman and his wife, however, were not the stuff of which managements were made, and seemed to find this hammed-up line from some play that was charitably happier forgotten, of stunning relevance. Their mouths dropped open. They uttered not a word. They stood and gaped as the centurion swept back his cloak, descended the steps and swaggeringly paused before our — at least, Smith Smith was obviously waiting for it — applause.

"Miss — ." It was a shaken plea for reassurance from Mr Everyman. "He's foreign. He's drunk."

"Might be drugs," Mrs Everyman muttered darkly. "You can never tell, these days."

Both of them eyed me hopefully, and I failed not, but stepped into the breach.

"It's all right, he's an actor. We're — um rehearsing a film, we're up from London." No need, I thought to bother about the exile far from his home, and the link with the refugees.

Their sighs of relief and gratification were loudly audible as their fascinated eyes swivelled as though on wires back to Smith Smith.

"*Pulchra*'s," he roared at me, leering harder than ever, and he attempted to land me a friendly punch on the shoulder that would have laid me flat except that I managed to side-step it neatly. "*Amici erimus.*"

The Everymans were by now extracting every shred of enjoyment they could from the proceedings. I could see words forming in their heads with which to regale their intimates with a story of which Smith Smith and I and the encounter on the walls would provide the kernel, as it were, of the nut. Much could be made

15

of this, I could see them thinking as they exchanged glances.

"Shut up, you fool," I hissed at Smith Smith, as his mouth opened again beneath the Roman helmet. "Clear off back to the hotel if you've finished shooting, for heaven's sake, don't get us all into trouble."

He pondered for a few seconds, then, as though in defiance, turned to his fascinated audience of Everymans and lifted his arm in a salute.

"Valete, tamen, amici," he bellowed, then turned and took off along the wall into the mist, much to my relief. When he had disappeared, the Everymans and I looked at each other. I was not in a giving vein, and my smile was slightly chilled.

"The film — ," began Missis rather breathlessly.

"It'll be advertised," I said, as one who dared not reveal more.

"But what's it going to be called? We won't want to miss that, will we, mother?"

Desperately, I opened my mouth.

"Exile", I found myself saying.

"Exile!"

16

Satisfaction evident in every line of their unisex macintoshes, they nodded at each other, nodded at me, and retreated in good order up the steps into the turret. The spiky Christmas tree was the last I saw of them, being manipulated sideways through the turret arch. I wondered what would happen when they passed Jon and Freddie further along, wherever they'd been shooting, but comforted myself with the thought that if Smith Smith had gone, the gear would be stowed away by now, and they'd be on their way back. I'd wait.

It seemed to be a long time and I was cold, stamping my feet and banging my hands together. I had just decided that I wouldn't wait any longer when I heard Jon's voice.

" — never knew he had it in him. That's why we got him cheap, I suppose, he's undiscovered talent."

"If you're referring to Smith Smith's personification of Mark Antony, as performed by our beloved Head Boy and pride of the school, I'm afraid I can't go along with that," I said, all melancholy, all cold forgotten at the sight

17

of Jon's face, his eyes warm and lit by the blue glow I loved more than my life.

"What, Roz? No, I was talking about the last shots we took, after he came back."

The snowflakes on my cheeks were gentle as a fleeting kiss.

"Came back?" I said interrogatively.

"Yes, we were going to pack up — it was hopeless, he was no use at all so we sent him off out of the cold — ."

"Now, I want to get this straight," I said. "Twenty minutes or so ago, yes? You packed up and sent him back — he came past on his way to the hotel — I saw him — have witnesses — ."

The Everymans would, I thought momentarily, be only too charmed to recount every detail of their historic meeting with the star of Exile.

" — and he did go to the hotel — I sent him back myself, he was making an exhibition of himself," I pursued briskly, lifting a glove to wipe away the snowflake kisses that were harder now, more (when I came to consider it) in keeping with the man who'd yelled *Pulchra*'s approvingly at me before trying to land me that

18

playful wallop on the shoulder.

"Oh no, he must have — well, changed his mind," said Jon, little realising that in those few words he had broken the barriers between what was real — the chilly greyness of a pre-Christmas day on the walls of Chester — and what the actual exile himself had thought about being sent far from his homeland.

"Not a word," Jon was continuing, hitching the weight of his case higher on his shoulder. "He just loomed up out of that bloody mist and stood by the wall, never looked at either of us, did he Freddie? And it was perfect — perfect — . All the loneliness, the drooping shoulders — you could practically see his thoughts — . That longing, the heart-sickness — . I didn't dare to say anything in case he moved — I shot off a whole film straight. And then he — where did he go, Freddie? I was busy with the camera."

"Dunno, mate. I was lighting a fag out of the wind. Into the nearest bar, I reckon, he knew you'd finished, he'd done his stuff."

I wondered for a wild moment whether

Smith Smith would ever know what a debt he owed to the legionnaires of Ancient Rome. There must, I deduced, have been a whole army of them watching with interest from the shadows of whatever plane those tough guys inhabited, eager to contribute.

"Where is he now?" I asked cautiously, assailed on all sides by flurrying snow-kisses that were both a recognition and a goodbye.

"Waiting for us in the warm, I expect. Come on love, let's go and celebrate. I've got the most fantastic pictures I've ever taken on that film. This is going to be the breakthrough for us, you'll see." Completely unaware, Jon took my arm.

There would be no point in asking our self-satisfied thespian exactly how or when he'd got back to the hotel, I knew. If he was hopeless at his art itself, he was compensatingly good at saying whatever blatant untruth he thought would ease his path to the stars with the direct honesty of a man whose word it was impossible to doubt.

I didn't want to know, though, I didn't want to spoil my private miracle. My heart was overflowing with love and associated emotions — but above all, gratitude. To them — those exiles who'd joined me in spirit on the walls when I'd felt myself lost, fighting for Jon's talent and integrity against the barbarian hordes of money-minded commercial sharks who didn't want truth and goodness and simplicity, but fake, sham, tinsel glitter.

I lifted my face to the sting of the snowflakes as we headed for home, in a gesture of acceptance. I didn't even have to wait until Jon developed that last film, to know that he was right — the pictures would be something special, very special.

But how special, how unbelievably and wonderfully special, only I — and the ghosts of those rough, lovely gents who'd spent their time tramping the walls of Chester in their legionnaires' boots — would ever know.

Summing up Aries — The Ram
(March 21 – April 20)

The self has a strong grip on challenges. Concern for other people will develop scope for philanthropy.

Your ability to take action will add your instinctive decisiveness to your drive for renewal.

Courage in the face of life's dooms will allow you to master your destiny and become a pioneer.

Resilience gives you the chance to take the initiative.

Leo excites you.

Libra teaches you.

Cancer signs can comfort you.

You carry the cosmic blueprint of your own sign.

Numbers with 9 in tend to be lucky.

Bloodstone, garnet and diamond are your stones and help you.

Cotton, stone and iron inspire you.

Lucky colours are reds, scarlets and crimsons.

Fires bring out your inner intensity.

Writing including sharp angles with tender forms brings out the finest in those you write to.

In health watch the face, muscles, head and upper mouth.

Pets can be fun if they are other people's. There can be competition if you feel a partner has a superior pet.

Although you like flowers, strong smelling herbs can be a source of joy to you too.

The thoughtlessness of others can bring out a combative quality in you. Some people find you a little brash. At times you appear selfish to others — this can bring mutual hostility.

Destruction of dreams and plans can result from too much aggressiveness. Those unable to appreciate your finer qualities will make crude comments about your naïve incomplete nature, as they see it. Find out where the true weaknesses lie.

Use Mars, the symbol of your planetary energy, to achieve your goals and persuade lesser beings to follow your leads.

Taurus
(April 21 – May 20)

THE signs of Taurus are Earth, Fixed, Negative. This is the sign of the builder; the principles of security and endurance are paramount. However this is not the sign of the architect — or initiator — and in this sense Taureans can on occasion be rather passive, because they are likely to follow an already-created pattern.

They will seek to preserve stability and harmony, and the love of beauty is strong. An emphasis on the external properties of beauty, however, can sometimes lead to a charge of greed.

Taureans are emotional and instinctive, with a subjective interest in maintaining the status quo because of a need for permanency: this can incur a violent reaction to change. Steadfastness of purpose, though, and the ability to withstand pressure, ensure that what flowers in Taurus remains evergreen.

Taureans seek things of lasting value. They desire to build then consolidate by establishing enduring stabilising activities with conservative but sometimes reactionary views.

Typical of their sign of the bull, they are determined to the point of obstinacy, though they will also be patient and stolid when pushed too far. At times they can be placid, lethargic and deliberately unimaginative. In an enterprising mood, however, Taureans can combine and adapt in a visionary fashion.

★ ★ ★

The story I have chosen to represent Taurus is SEASON OF GIVING. In this, the central character illustrates many of the attributes of the typical Taurean — she is concerned about material security (though in her case, very justifiably) and does not want change. She celebrates the old ways with her gesture at the end, and in her relationships, reveals the Taurean characteristics of possessiveness and stubbornness. However, her steadfast nature will, we have

no doubt, bring her safely through her
period of difficulty.

Season of Giving

It was just gone seven o'clock on
Christmas Eve, bitter cold but not
snowing, when there was a loud knock
on the door. Gwena crossed the room in
a panic, the flickering firelight throwing
her shadow round her on three walls
— she hadn't lit the oil lamp, oil was
a luxury and the fire lit the room well
enough, softening the shabbiness of the
furniture with its red glow.

"Who is it?" she called loudly, her
hand on the bolt of the door.

There was a pause, then a muffled
voice said: "Me. Jack."

Gwena's gaze flew to Branwen, lying
on the old horsehair sofa, covered over
with the quilt from the bed upstairs
and her old fur fabric coat, for extra
warmth.

Upstairs in the bedroom, Gwena knew,
the paper was peeling off the walls with
the damp. The back of the cottage stood

against earth, cut away to a lower level, and from the road outside you could touch the slates on the roof if you reached over the low wall.

Ill though Branwen was, Gwena couldn't let her stay in that icy room upstairs. She'd carried her down the stairs and put her on the sofa, drawn it round to the fire, covered her over with everything there was. And at last, worn out with her cough, Branwen was sleeping.

Gwena's face was pinched and thin, like that of a frightened mouse, and her hair was prematurely grey. Her hands fluttered indecisively.

She pulled back the bolt and opened the door. He was muffled up in a fur-collared coat, a dark bulk against the starry sky and the outline of the old cherry tree.

"I thought you weren't in. Sitting in the dark, eh?"

She held the door open for him to enter. As he walked into the room, bending his head to avoid the beam, she said stiffly: "I'll light the lamp."

He was peering round, half-humorous,

half-incredulous. "What the — ? Oh, is this — ?"

Gwena scurried round. "She's not well, she's been coughing something awful, but I've had the doctor to her, and he says she'll be all right — ."

Against his drawling voice, her own sounded sharper and more Welsh than ever. She couldn't help but be aware, although she wasn't unduly sensitive, of his uneasiness as he looked at the child, her black curls tangled round her flushed face, the old fur fabric tucked round her shoulders.

He tried to sound genial. "Not well? Got a cough and ill for Christmas?"

"Always been delicate, she has," said Gwena stubbornly.

Jack stared round the shabby room. There were no decorations, no Christmas Tree. Only some holly on the sideboard. Holly from the garden didn't cost anything.

He was uncomfortable. He looked back at Gwena, and she returned his stare fiercely.

"I didn't — realise," he began.

"What, may I ask?"

28

"That you might be needing — things."

"We don't need nothing. We've got our bit of dinner for tomorrow in, and a cake and all."

"But — ." He gestured round awkwardly. "This place — ."

"And what's wrong with it?" Gwena didn't look like a mouse now, she looked and sounded like a shrew.

Jack didn't dare to say that it was disgraceful, that it was a hovel and not fit to live in.

"I — er — I brought — ." He couldn't get Branwen's name out. " — the little girl a present. It's in the car."

Gwena didn't relax.

"I'll get it," he said, and left the room hurriedly.

The door closing disturbed the sleeping child, and she stirred. "Mam — ."

"Be, cariad?" Gwena was at her side jealously, smoothing the hair back from her hot forehead. "Be t'eisio?"

But Branwen clutched her mother's hand, coughed once, and then drifted back to sleep. Gwena tucked the fur fabric round her. The old building was full of draughts.

Jack was subdued when he returned, and when she saw what he was carrying, she understood why. It was an enormous doll, dressed in silk and lace — better clothed than either Gwena or Branwen.

He had the grace to look ashamed as he handed it over. The lamp had turned the red glow of the room to yellow, and in its soft light he wouldn't meet her eyes.

"If you — ." He cleared his throat. "If there's anything — ."

"Well?" She was daring him to say it.

He made a show of glancing at the old clock on the sideboard. "Good God, is that the time? I must be getting back — didn't realise it was so late — ."

"The kettle's boiling. Have a cup of tea before you go."

But he wouldn't hear of it — she'd understand — pressures — got to get back — . As he stood poised in the doorway, pulling up his collar against the cold, and the sharp air whirled into the room, Jack glanced back at the huddled figure on the sofa. Gwena wondered whether he might ask to kiss Branwen.

"Well, all the best." The relief of

getting out of an awkward situation was in his voice. "If there's anything — er — ."

The expression on her face stopped him. "Good night," she said.

And he was gone. The door was shut and they were alone in the yellow lamplight. The fire had gone low, and mechanically, Gwena went over and stooped to poke it, behind the thick black bars of the old grate. She added a few lumps of her carefully-hoarded coal, and then sat down in the chair with its familiar sagging springs.

She'd done what she thought was right and yet, with his presence still lingering in the room, all she could feel was hopelessness. Branwen needed good food, a warm coat — the coal might not last — . You couldn't, Gwena thought bitterly, live on pride.

A sound outside the door brought her out of her reverie with a start. Scuffling and giggling, and then tremolo voices plunging into the high notes of *We Three Kings of Orient Are*, erratically wandering from key to key, to the accompaniment of an enthusiastic but

31

inaccurate mouth-organ.

They'd manage, of course they would! They always had, hadn't they? There was the washing, and Mrs Maggie Hughes at The Shop kindness itself — .

Gwena threw another piece of coal, a big one, onto the fire, and then got up. There were things to do. The doll must be put away in the sideboard so that Branwen wouldn't see it until the morning. There was — .

An inspired thought struck her, swept through her, and became an obsession. She'd give the carol-singers — yes, she would! — she'd give them (it was the Morgan children from along the road) — she'd give them a whole shilling!

She took the lid off the biscuit tin in the drawer, and fumbled for the coin, her mouse mouth working with fierce joy. That would show him!

Summing up Taurus
(April 21 – May 20)

Taurus the Bull. Your ruling planet is Venus.

Lucky number 6.

Lucky colour: Blue.

Lucky gemstone: Rose quartz.

Herb: Sage.

Tree: Birch.

Element: Earth.

You always possess some passion, practicality, loyalty, perseverance, determination.

You are often self-indulgent and stubborn.

Your career, goals and vocation will include: Comfortable surroundings achieved by patience and your hard work brings results.

You do not like to be hurried but are always open to new things.

You are sensual.

You are sometimes too rigid but once you have learned a few skills you can achieve a great deal with them.

You achieve a good deal of emotional healing through your feelings of self-worth.

Meditation (to be undertaken either with or without a stone held in the left hand):

Hold your muscles in then relax.

Breathe out negativity and stress.

Dissipate unwanted thoughts.
Allow love in.
Prayer:
May the wisdom of Minos allow the noble thoughts to flow through the healing horns into your body and out into your environment.
Light a blue candle and repeat 6 times:
I am worthy of the spiritual path.
Grant me the power to provide shelter for those in need.
My image lifts my emotions out of the mother earth into the hills.
Let the sage give me knowledge to heal.
May the magic of mind lift my spirit to heaven.

Gemini
(May 21 – June 21)

AIR, Mutable, Positive. You are the first sign of Mind — ie you are a 'psychological' sign. This is the key to your mutability, or your ability to accommodate change, as it is Mind that can rationalise the permutations, the ups and downs, of circumstance.

Beware of vanity, though, which can often lead you into superficiality, especially when nothing is consolidated before moving on: the desire for change, instead of what change really means, can become more important to you.

You have much inquisitiveness, scope and communicative ability, though all this emphasis on Mind can sometimes overload the mental faculty and create deviation and eccentricity. Your acute perceptive powers bring you a heightened awareness of the duality inherent in human nature — the Gemini 'twins' — often giving rise to an instinctive feel towards environment and atmosphere.

Sun in Gemini natives tend towards the establishment of relationships. There is a strong desire for awareness. In work lifestyle you are able via improving communications, to add a sense of logic. You are good at imitation, jazzing up inventions and assisting with reasoning and learning. Your adaptability carried to the point of instability should be used to adapt to events.

Although you are constantly alert, impatience can lead to experimental restlessness. You are suggestible as well as being inquisitive. You can be gay and joyful and yet be superficial and inconsistent, thus diffusing the admiration felt for you by others.

Your skills are concentration alternating with relaxation, giving you the power to organise while simply appearing to listen.

★ ★ ★

The story which illustrates Gemini is called SHADOW PLAY.

This story illustrates how the soul or

36

sun energy of Gemini combines with the mind to produce a victory from apparent defeat. Mercury is the ruler of Gemini and this planet has to do with the mind, even when there is an apparent loss of mental facilities. The negative Gemini can be stubborn and conceited; this can cause all forms of study, effort and business to downgrade.

In this story the heroine's lack of optimism leads to a realistic approach with a final survival. If the mind had been too inflexible, dogmatism and prejudice could have won over.

Conflicts of direction and goals allow the heroine to stop and stare long enough to think. What could have led to emotional disturbance through inner pressures is altered in a restless instability that nervously cuts through the underhanded threat of the situation. Damaging inconsistency is turned via excitability and hypochondria to an outcome with the Gemini spell of eccentric meditation.

Thus some inactivity and lack of common sense help the unnamed heroine to shrug off her own lack of contentment.

What could have been viewed as a potential legal problem or a vulnerability to deception is transformed. Ironically the lack of the ability to communicate produces a sort of fugue that resists insensitivity or an overly critical attitude to cut through ignorance.

There was an unexpected productivity here that enhanced intelligence. The persuasions were freed of all prejudice to arrive at a peaceful state. Caution and pride joined forces to provide an ability to relate to another. The forcefulness of the will was such that the future could more precisely be predicted. An act of compassion led to a knowledge of the self.

Shadow Play

Sitting in the deep bay window that juts out over where the steps go down to the sea. High tide, it seems to lap at the very foundations of the house, each ebb and flow wearing away the solid rock so that I can see, almost in an eye-blink, that eternal patience crumbling the last fragment, the house collapsing, being swallowed up. Or only the echo of the house. It won't be there then.

Now, though, it is present, it is real. Window-seat with padded chintz cushions supports me; glass is cold against my nose; velvet hangings are soft to my touch. I look at my hand, lifted to stroke the claret-coloured draperies. My hand. This strange, bony appendage with blue veins and gawky knuckles. It doesn't look like my hand, but it is. I exist. I live. This is my hand, I tell myself.

I stare at it for a few moments, wondering, then let it drop, pick up the pen and notebook beside me and turn from the grey day outside, the fog heavy with fine droplets of water that cling to the window panes, the presence of the sea muted, invisible. Here there is warmth, the reassurance of thick red carpets, the spaciousness of the high ceiling, the cream walls with mirrors catching the light in prisms and throwing it back and forth, from side to side.

TODAY, THE FUTURE STARTS

I pause, consider the words I have written. It depends whether you have a positive or a negative attitude. Today is the watershed, the line between what has gone and what will come. Today the future starts, but today, equally certainly, the past ends. Unborn tomorrow, said Omar, and dead yesterday. And in between, the shifting seconds of now.

I rise, go across to one of the mirrors, stare at myself with impersonal curiosity. How boring to see the same face every time I look in a mirror. I twist my head to try and catch an angle of myself that I have never seen before, some small glimpse to relieve the dullness bred by familiarity. It doesn't work. It never works. Always the same me that looks back.

How old is my face? Time means nothing to the soul. Age is just a word. Every year of my life I have looked different, but to myself I am always the same. Trapped in the now of the present. Maybe even memory is an illusion. I think about Time. The ticking of my watch, the beat of my heart. On and on, for ever and ever. Yet each tick,

40

each beat, is the only one that exists. The last has slipped into the past; the next may never happen. How slender is the thread. We live always in the moment of awareness. What is real may change by the time we draw another breath. Where was I, a heart-beat ago? Now I am here, but where was I then? I cling to the reality of my own pulse, afraid in sudden panic that it may stop. I feel the blood pounding in my head so that I can see nothing. Feel the dimensions sliding from my grasp. Run from the room in smothering terror, calling:

"Edwin. Edwin?"

Where the hell is he? Anger stabs through me. He should be here when I need him. He's here often enough when I don't, when I want to be left alone. Hovering, protecting, caring, until I could scream.

His voice floats up from the depths of the hall below the wide, shallow stair-case.

"Is that you, pigeon?"

Emerging from the study doorway, bald head shining, shirt-sleeves neatly confined by old-fashioned gold cuff-links, brown spaniel's eyes watching me anxiously as I go down the stairs.

"Is something the matter?"

The reality of smooth wood under my hands has brought me back. The terror is gone, and the anger is taking on form. It's settled on Edwin's baldness, his stockiness, and especially the concern in his eyes. I feel such revulsion that I know I have to get away.

"I thought I'd go for a walk," I say, through stiff lips.

"In this fog?" he says doubtfully, just as I knew he would. Irritation sharpens my voice. This is a familiar ritual.

"Why shouldn't I go for a walk?"

He sighs.

"I'm busy at the moment, but I'll come for a walk with you later."

Is it worth the effort of arguing, asserting myself? This morning, I haven't got the strength. I say nothing.

"Why don't you go and do some writing?" he suggests, and mutely, heavy-limbed, I turn and begin the climb to the top floor and the cliché Edwin's faithfully observed — the attic converted into a 'work-room' where I have spread out my papers and books, typewriter and pen. Stiff with resentment, I shut the door behind me, reject Edwin, reject the world. I don't want to write. I feel tired, exhausted. I sit on the big patchwork cushion on the floor, lean against the wall, curl myself up small, think about living and dying.

★ ★ ★

Man, said Rousseau, is born free, but is everywhere in chains. Huddled on the cushion, I wonder about freedom, about chains. Was I born free? A free spirit with free will? Or was it all predestined, my path laid out for me? Were the chains already waiting even as I was laid in Maeve's arms for the first time? Could I have broken away, smashed the bonds that linked me in my small dependency to the two creatures who had fashioned my earthly body from their own?

Could I have piped infant defiance into Maeve's face or denied those other hands, that, in their male strength, protected his child from scavengers? Should I have somehow realised the enormity of his crime, recognised the dark wings beating round my head when, a scavenger himself, he swooped from the clouds to violate, even as the tears streamed down his face, the flesh of his own living lamb?

The weakness was in him, not in me, yet it was round the mind of his child that the chains grew tighter, the trap closed. Should I have, with atavistic wisdom beyond my years, passed judgement on him, pronounced sentence, cut through my chains with an epigram and left him kneeling, shamed yet still assured of his soul's salvation if he confessed in humility the frailties of his flesh?

"Mea culpa," he weeps, through his fingers, his gaze turned inward to the dark, secret, ecstatic sin. And Maeve beside him, her hair a cloud, the nails of a martyr's cross bleeding from her unseeing eyes where they have pierced the soul and life is dripping away.

"Mea culpa." Maeve forms the words with her lips.

For them the richness of the ruby lamp, gold stars, penitence thick as incense on the air, abasement, chastisement, absolution. But the unspoken reality grows in the womb of their child like a monstrous cancer, until the time comes when it breaks forth into hideous form, splitting the shell that has carried the burden for so long.

Red slashes across my wrists released that devouring spectre of guilt into my own image, my shadow, my shape, my doppelganger. It was a confrontation sealed with blood. "I am you and you are me. You can never escape me. I will never leave you." I can see her clearly, myself, my other self, her white skin charred, festering. She is laughing across from the mirror, even as I hide my eyes. I can hear her laughter beating from the four walls, beating me down, battering me to the floor.

"Let me die. Oh, God, let me die."

But instead I feel those familiar hands that fathered both her and me, a travesty of tenderness. I hear Maeve's scream splintering the air into a million shattered pieces. God is Love. Love is his hands, his lips, his voice, and Maeve's prostrate body weeping tears that will never end for my soul. Love is the stain of my guilt, the image in the mirror that haunts me as I run from room to room, the sin that laughs down the corridors of memory like a scratched old record on the turntable of Time, playing itself in my head until I beat myself again and again at the floor so that my pain may silence it.

God is Love. God is Infinite. God is everywhere. There is no escape. But later comes the cleansing, the purging of my spirit. The realisation that I can leap the bounds of reality, forsake the substance for the shadow. I can see through the mirror. I see Lucifer strong and magnificent, the throne of God beneath him shrivelling. I see that black is white, that dark is light, that day is night. I am Judas, giving the kiss of love to my betrayer. I know myself, I am the image behind the glass, I am the alter ego cast by the sun, that runs on the ground and crawls with the worms. Nothing can confine me. I have found my freedom.

★ ★ ★

Chained then, but I am free as air. I am travelling from nowhere into nothing. I have no roots to pull me down. I never speak of the house in London, I do not want to remember it. And I have denied Maeve's memories of Ireland, wiped out the sound of her voice as, a third in our dark trinity, she mourned that I had tempted him, that I made him fall. I have rejected the prayers that insinuated themselves into my dreams, the earnest pleading for my salvation.

Maeve blamed herself because that was in her nature, and she blamed me because I was the reincarnation of that self, but not wispy and insubstantial, something formed from the mists and glimmers on lake water, dimmed through hours on her knees, weeping. I was the Maeve she might have been once, hair softly curling round white shoulders, eyes with their sooty lashes so deeply blue that they smote your heart. Not a wraith, but a vivid and vital being of fire, an enchantress. She never blamed him. It was her fault, and it was mine, because I was her daughter and in spite of my unawareness, my innocence, the pattern played itself through a second time, and once again he was too weak to resist.

So I have no country. I am a wanderer. I can go where I please and do what I will. There is no Time for me. I regulate it myself, create my own days and nights.

Here, though, in this house, Edwin's reality rules me, as it did in the house in Hampstead where he and Mrs Edwards and the ghost of his mother had established their rituals long before he married me. Edwin and Mrs Edwards and the ghost of his mother cling maniacally to the chains of their lives. Familiar. Comfortable. A place for everything, and everything in its place. An evening for cleaning the silver, which must never vary. After I broke a cup from the Doulton tea-service, I was not allowed to wash up again.

"You don't need to, pigeon. Mrs Edwards would rather do it, as she has always done. You don't need to do anything."

"But Edwin, I'd like to think I was being useful."

His smile, indulging a child.

"You're a writer, you don't have to be useful. And after all, you're not strong yet, you've got to get well. I'll see to everything. Just don't you worry your head about anything except your poems."

Smothering, feeling the weight of yet another love grinding me down, stifling me, I accepted the burden and nodded. How hard is resignation when one's protest is not against evil but good; not against injustice but benevolence; not against starvation but a surfeit of sweetness.

In spite of his love for me, his devotion, even my physical presence is an intrusion. His mother's ghost still presides over the household. The mahogany-and-stuffed-velvet chairs that stand round the table in the dining-room looking out over the sea, stood just so in the Hampstead house. The mirrors on the walls are filed with her image, her secretive smile. Mrs Edwards unfailingly washes, cleans, tidies as though a phantom finger will be run across surfaces looking for dust, a phantom frown pucker that imperious brow if there is a single deviation from the ritual established in the hollow, claret-draped rooms of the Hampstead house when, a red-cheeked wench from the country, Clara Dew as she was then, she tearfully attempted to accept her new life 'in service'.

After a while, her longing for green fields and apple blossom quivering in the spring sunlight, laughter in crystal droplets like spilled water from the pump, faded. Maybe there was a renewal of life when she managed to become Clara Edwards; maybe she hoped the colours would come back into her world of coal-scuttles and blacking and morning teas served behind heavy drawn curtains, the egg boiled for exactly two-and-a-half minutes, or else the spoon would be laid down without comment, but there would be no escaping the accusation in those eyes.

Maybe, but the face that smiles from the frame in her room, cap tilted jauntily as though to defy Air Force Regulations, was blown to pieces over the Channel. Sometimes Mrs Edwards plays Vera Lynn singing 'We'll Meet Again' and 'The White Cliffs of Dover' on her old cabinet gramophone, and enjoys an evening of tearful nostalgia. But using the right serving spoons with the vegetable dishes brings more balm to Mrs Edwards's soul than anticipating reunion with the laughing-eyed and shattered face within the frame.

A sea-gull has alighted noisily outside the little gable window, on the sill, taking me by surprise. Even as I gasp at the sudden violation of my peace, it struts, crying, and I exist in the now, the room taking substance round me.

I laugh, scramble to my feet, go across to pull faces at the gull. Beyond the window, the fog swirls. I am aware of the sound of the sea. Images flash through my brain. Red velvet turns to silver and palest green; upholstered chairs become unicorns tossing their manes like smoke upon the air — .

And then the sound of the Tyrolean cow-bell that hangs in the hall echoes through the house. Mrs Edwards is telling us that lunch is ready. I am ravenous. I run down the stairs while the bell still vibrates. I am alive and life is suddenly very good.

Edwin is sitting at the round table in the dining-room. Dishes on the snowy cloth sizzle invitingly. The glasses and knives catch the grey light. The room is full of small rainbows, and I feel so bursting with power that I could catch them in my hands. Edwin holds out my chair, seats himself opposite to me. We smile at each other, while we pile chops and vegetables onto the gold-rimmed plates.

"Well, have you finished your work?" Teasing him.

"Yes, pigeon, all done." His soft brown eyes rest on me with love. I look away hastily, beginning to eat.

"Did you write anything?" he asks.

"No, but I saw a sea-gull. It landed on the window-sill. It was a good idea to come here, wasn't it? Better than London. More elemental; you can feel the world turning."

Edwin chews his food thoughtfully, a slight frown between his brows. I try to repair the breach.

"I mean, you haven't cut yourself off completely. Just semi-retired. And the rest of the time you can relax. Not feel so pressured."

"No."

I want to tell him about the rainbows within the reach of my hands, the consciousness in this now, this moment, of El Dorado somewhere beyond the boom of the sea as the tide swirls below us, the glittering apples of the Hesperides lost in the mist outside the window. I can feel the longing to speak like a lump in my throat. I have difficulty in swallowing. I try to say something that will reach him.

"Shall we go for a walk after lunch, then?"

"If you would like to."

It is impossible. But I try again.

"I'm thinking of the flowers hidden under all this fog. The crocuses are coming out now, you know, they always remind me of jewels, so bright. The pink shrub's got loads of blossoms — I think it's an azalea — but they're white aren't they? — or it might be a camellia — oh, the romance of Marguerite Gautier — how lovely if we've got our own camellia — ."

Edwin grimaces suddenly.

53

"I'll have to tell Mrs Edwards to mash the potatoes in future, they're repeating on me."

I shut my eyes momentarily. When I open them, I look for the rainbows knowing they will be gone. El Dorado is an echo of old fables, dead men's tales from beyond the Pillars of Hercules. The Hesperides, shores of the Isles of the Blessed, were never there at all. The fog weeps outside the window.

I eat the food and taste nothing. My hands move stiffly, like those of an automaton. Edwin talks about share prices. I nod, a half-smile fixed to my mouth. The silver scrapes on the gold-rimmed plates.

"Edwin," I say desperately, "What day is it?"

"Wednesday, pigeon."

I'll hold onto Wednesday. And when we go for our walk, I know his hand will be there, his fingers gentle, possessive of mine. I'll have the stone flags of the path solid beneath my feet. The lilac bush by the gate will be dripping moisture. There's a road outside and the gulls will be calling.

I will ask Mrs Edwards for some bread. Give it to the gulls.

Summing up Gemini
(May 21 – June 21)

Fortunate day: Wednesday.
Lucky colour: orange.
Lucky gem: agate. The agate is a stone which harmonises and balances physical and mental health, the body and mind.
Ruling planet: Mercury.
The constellation of Gemini is often known as 'The Twins'. They were Castor and Pollux, in old mythology, the sons of Leda the Swan. Milton referred to them as the 'Ledean stars'. Castor is a Fixed Alpha star representing the mortal twin, while the Beta star is Pollux, held to be immortal. There is a similar Egyptian legend relating to Horus the Elder and Horus the Younger, twins who were born to the goddess Isis.
Gemini is often given the lucky number 5, but Inner Circle astrologers point out the link with the number 72, the number of genii in the Seals of Solomon.

Gemini is often linked with the lungs and hence the permanent rhythmic bond which the human being holds to the outer world, constantly taking in air and oxygen so that what is inside becomes outside, and what is outside becomes inside.

Some Geminis favour smooth grey fabrics, indicating their need to relate to others.

Cancer
(June 22 – July 23)

SUN in Cancer seeks emotional growth, though due to romantic attachments you may become clannish. While you seek to nurture and protect, you can be somewhat reticent about your own deeper feelings. When you are moody you could be described as cautious, timid, self-pitying.

With others you can be gregarious, while as a parent you are exacting and may be perceived as shrewd and niggling.

Your sensitive touchy nature can be quelled by logic lovingly applied, leading eventually to more emotional stability while retaining a healthy imagination and tenacity.

Sun in Cancer is Water, Cardinal, Negative. Like your emblem, the Crab, you can acquire an outer shell of resilience with a vulnerable interior. This can sometimes produce displays of bravado, though in fact you are a real softy. People often call you sentimental, and this feature is perhaps best expressed by your feelings for the historical past: you respect things antique for their traditional pedigree. This leads to a sympathy for the inner nature of things, and an openness to the idea of 'soul'.

Moodiness can become a negative outlet for 'soulful' feelings. You have much personal enterprise and resourcefulness, though these can make you at times perhaps too self-concerned. But resourcefulness — and an instinctive compassion — can incline you to be generous in giving others the benefit of your inner — spiritual — nature.

★ ★ ★

The story I have chosen to illustrate the sign of Cancer is SIXPENCE. Here there are many threads running through the life of the heroine. She is deeply sentimental and romantic, though she keeps her inner feelings very much to herself — she is too proud to show how her soul can be touched.

She is also linked on many levels to

her family — she has cared for them and nurtured them, she treasures the little trinkets that have marked family life over the years. She has allowed herself to grow into a model of what her family would have wanted her to be — and yet we see in this story the emergence, much later on in her life, of the child she was, her own individual and distinct personality, which is going to produce out of the past, the one consolation that will soothe the heart of the woman she is now.

Sixpence

She'd managed to keep calm all through discussing the hymns John would have wanted, the details of the service, though it nearly proved too much when she asked for Elgar's 'Nimrod' to be played as the mourners went in. He'd so loved Elgar, she doubted whether she'd be able to listen to the swelling, soaring beauty that brought John's long figure in the wing chair, his head tilted, eyes closed, listening, to vivid life before her, without screaming, tearing her hair, going wild with the frenzy of her grief. Gone! Gone for ever! Nevermore — nevermore — .

She swallowed, and turned a dry-eyed, composed face to a catalogue of some sort that was being held out to her by the softly-spoken man in the dark suit. The horror of it hit her like a blow. Would she like to choose the coffin? The professionally sympathetic voice droned in her ears. Wood — handles — the words twined themselves into shapes that seemed to fill the air of the summer afternoon, mingle with the scent of the roses from the garden, smite her tired brain from all directions. The coffin — the coffin — the coffin — . She shut her eyes, retreated from the tasteful room, the slanting sunlight on the rose-beds outside, to another summer, another hot afternoon, a child standing in a cotton frock, battered sandals on her dusty bare feet, hair falling tangled round the thin little face, staring at something that winked and sparkled on the worn surface of the country road.

Sixpence! Vanny peered closer to be sure she wasn't dreaming. A whole sixpence! Her pocket money for a week!

60

What a wonderful, unbelievable gift from the gods! She'd found sixpence!

She leaned over and grabbed it, clutching it tightly in her hot, sticky hand, already in her mind's eye within the confines of The Shop, choosing between chocolate — a whole bar if she wanted — or the big gob stoppers that changed colour as you sucked them, turning from purple to green, yellow, violent orange. But the cherry lips, she must have some cherry lips, they were her most favouritest of all — perhaps cherry lips and dolly mixtures — . Then she remembered that it was early closing day. The Shop would be shut!

Oh, tragedy! The unfairness of it was so crushing she didn't think she'd survive until tomorrow, and by then, all the wonder of being able to spend her precious sixpence would have gone. She wanted to spend it now, now, to be able to go and sit at the end of the garden and gorge herself on cherry lips and dolly mixtures and jelly babies. If she was sick tomorrow, it wouldn't matter, tomorrow was years and years away, she wanted all the joys *now*. Her sixpence burned furiously at her palm, the edge digging into her fingers, crying: "Spend me! Spend me!"

Then in a wild and wonderful second, lightning struck with recollection that was so much of a relief that she almost fell over. Her heart began to beat again. Mrs Thomas, of course. Old Mrs Thomas who lived in the cottage behind all those rustling dark rhododendron bushes at the end of Top Lane, alone except for her cats, whose front parlour was piled up with boxes of mysterious things like candles and bootlaces. Who kept a row of big glass jars with bulls eyes and toffee and sticky peppermints in them, and an old-fashioned pair of scales to painstakingly weigh out the ounces.

Vanny's feet were away before she could remind herself that she didn't like the gloomy rustling of the rhododendrons, that the cats were vicious and one of them had once scratched her when she tried to stroke it, that Mrs Thomas — she was certain — was a witch, with her white hair and eyes like jet buttons, hard and unblinking, and her sunken mouth with one tooth that stuck out.

No wonder there had never, to Vanny's recollection, ever been a Mr Thomas. He had run away, like she would if she had to live in that smelly house with the cats sitting everywhere, and the witch stumping in and out of the tiny dark rooms. Or perhaps — she could feel her feet slowing on the upward climb to Top Lane, the sky was getting dark, keeping company with the gathering darkness of her thoughts — the witch had poisoned him, boiled a witch's brew over the fire and chuckled fiendishly as she forced the spoon between his unwilling lips, the way Mother sometimes took her by surprise when she had to swallow the cold liver oil she hated. She didn't really want to brave the fears of the rhododendrons and the cats and the witch — did she? But then she felt the sixpence sweaty and metallic against her palm. Spend me, Spend me! She tried to think of liquorice sticks and toffee whirls — bars and bars of chocolate — and, beginning to catch her breath because of the hill, she plodded gamely on, feeling the air press down on her, heavy and sultry. Far off, thunder rumbled.

The rhododendrons were massive now, their leaves spotted with yellow so that they looked like something out of a nightmare. Vanny hung back, then summoning all her courage, ran through the dark tunnel between them, up the crooked stone path, with branches catching at her frock, twining in her hair and trying to hold her. Her heart was thumping painfully in her throat, almost choking her, she felt her eyes darting with terror every way at once. The thunder rumbled again, and she whimpered.

The front door stood open. Vanny hovered, clutching her sixpence hard against her like a magic talisman. Something shot out at her and she screamed shrilly. The yellow cat spat back, its back arched. Huge drops of rain fell, like pennies darkening the dust of the neglected garden. One fell on Vanny's head, making her jump with the sudden coldness through her hair. The trees seemed to be closing in on her, and she stumbled out of the eerie unnatural twilight into the cavern of the front parlour.

In the gloom, as she stood there

breathing hard, waiting for the witch to come in from the kitchen, she could hear rustling and small sounds in the dark corners. Shapes moved. Vannie's terror gripped her limbs. Monsters! Something touched her leg, and the paralysis snapped. It was the cats — the cats — . Only the cats.

Everything was so quiet she could hear her breath, ragged and gasping, hear the beat of her heart. So still. No sound only the cats as they padded softly round the room, their eyes catching the dim light, glowing sudden as green and yellow flames, and as briefly extinguished. Vannie felt a new fear, something she couldn't have explained. Why was it so quiet? Where was the witch?

Summoning strength to move, she took a step forward, and managed to call in a high little voice: "Mrs Thomas?"

Her foot touched a strange softness that moved, and Vannie jumped back, staring frantically down. Something dark — a dark shadow on the linoleum floor — but not moving now, only if she touched it with her foot. It was so very still, so very quiet. It was the witch lying on the floor, her white hair a blur against the blackness of her old-fashioned dress, her arm thrown out. Beside her, beneath her, were the shattered remains of a glass jar, bulls eyes staring up at Vannie with a million accusing gazes. She stared back, the hair lifting on her neck, prickles of unnameable, atavistic dread seizing her body, her mouth suddenly dry.

Tried to moisten her lips. Whispered: "Mrs Thomas?"

Nothing moved, only the cats, padding. There was no sound. No sound at all.

Then a brilliant flash of lightning illuminated the room with a sulphuric starkness, and as the thunder crashed and rolled about her, Vannie screamed, breaking the spell, whirled and fled down the tunnel of rhododendrons, unseeing, unknowing. Down the lane, down the hill, her fear-spurred feet carried her to the place where she knew nothing could touch her, and she pushed open the door to Mr Amos's workshop with her last remaining strength, and, hair dripping from the rain, frock clinging, feet soaked, sank trembling onto the stool beside the big black stove that swallowed coal in the winter and belched reassuringly with warmth and reassuring comfort.

"Can I polish some handles for you, Mr Amos?"

Forget the silence of that small dim parlour, forget the vigilant cats, their eyes winking messages she didn't understand, and — oh, most of all, forget the shape on the floor, the stillness, the hand reaching into nothing. Forget. Forget.

When she polished the handles, they shone like suns, she breathed on them and rubbed them energetically. Outside, the rain had stopped, the storm was over. Everywhere was dripping, beginning to steam, the sun was shining again. Think of sun — only sun — warm, bright. And Mr Amos's twinkling eyes as he admired her handiwork. As he always did when she came to the workshop wanting to help.

"Like to see what we've been making this afternoon, Jim and me?"

She'd never been allowed to see before, not the real thing, only the pieces of wood being planed and smoothed. She followed him to the door and looked into the inner room of the workshop.

It was beautiful. Just beautiful. The wood lovingly finished, the brass handles shining.

"Oh!" Vannie sighed. "I would so love to buy a coffin, Mr Amos." With belated recollection of what she had screwed up in the pocket of her frock, she added hopefully: "I've got sixpence."

Mrs Myfanwy Rhineheart rose from her chair, asked the man in the dark suit to wait for a moment, and went up to the room that had been hers and John's. Now hers. She had never spent that sixpence. She had carried it with her always, as a good luck piece. It was in the small jewel box where she kept her treasures. Not jewellery, but the things that marked milestones in her life. The first flower John had given her for a corsage, carefully pressed; her son's lock of baby hair; her mother's wedding ring, given to her by her father after the funeral. Slowly, she picked up the small coin, dulled with age, held it for a moment as she had held it those many years ago. Closed the box and put it back in the drawer. Went steadily down the stairs. The dark man was still there with his catalogue, but she gently pushed his hand to one side.

Holding out the sixpence, the healing tears coming at last, she said through the mist:

"I'll have the best. The very best coffin there is."

Summing up Cancer
(June 22 – July 23)

Lucky day: Monday.

Lucky stone: Moonstone, silver items, tectite, diamond, crystal, opal, beryl, mother of pearl. Any whitish stones are good.

Number — 2.

Love oils: Camphor and frankincense.

Herb: Sweet fern.

Mixing with others:

Water Sign — You are of a tender and sympathetic disposition, and you flow into other signs' hearts and minds. Try not to be too defensive.

Cardinal — You like to achieve things in your career: relationships must progress or you tend to discard them.

Money — You are tenacious and can be thrifty when you find a good reason for saving.

Cancer children like to be cuddled and loved. The vitality of the young Cancer child is charming.

You are easily hurt by a thoughtless word or deed.

Emotional security is vital to you now as then.

Although outwardly adventurous you can appreciate moral, emotional and physical support.

You can be fascinated by how things work.

Shyness is overcome so that you can experience the joys and sorrows of life acting in a forward, extrovert way.

You are in the prime of life in your early thirties onwards.

Leo
(July 24 – August 23)

SUN in Leo feels the desire for creative self expression. Dignity and vanity are important to you. You enjoy life and inspire it in others. You enjoy organising social events, bringing enthusiasm and a sense of pageantry to your efforts.

You have moods when you are exceptionally flamboyant. You can be very altruistic: it is a good idea to temper this with thrift, leaving yourself the time for material resources and to attend to fine details.

Moon in Leo. You are a romantic who loves the high life. Your dream is to live among the rich and famous, and you crave the accompanying life style. Because you love excitement you may have a tendency to create dramatic situations.

The dykes burst. The waterwheel turns.

71

Sun in Leo. Fire, Fixed, Positive.

You are the Sun Sign au naturelle in the sense that the sun itself is your own emblem. Accordingly, generous outpourings of feeling acquire for you the same value as the rays of the sun: you rightly see these as agencies of warmth and regeneration. However, like the sun you can become on occasion self-centred, sometimes leading others to charge you with being inconsiderate, perhaps even egotistical.

But the notion of individualism comes into its own in Leo, for it is natural for you to perceive the individual as being separate from the group force in its own right. Grand gestures are thus admired for their flourish and display of individual skill.

Children, because they live by the rules of the heart, will often warm to you, in that they will respond to your sunny nature.

★ ★ ★

My story for Leo is A QUESTION OF PATERNITY, which cleverly illustrates

72

both the negative and the positive aspects of this sign. Richard is obviously a Leo who has wandered from his rightful path, and who has allowed himself to become far more self-centred than is good for him.

The situation stirs him from his complacency on all levels, both physical and emotional. If a Leo allows his natural warmth to become repressed or channelled only into taking care of himself, the result can be a negative way of living which is all the more tragic because it is not in the natural way of events for this warm and golden sign. Losses are thus all the greater for both himself and those around him.

Happily, the sad events which lead up to the action of this story result in the breaking forth, after a traumatic climax, of the real emotional bounty of this Leo's sun, with the promise that the summer of his existence has only just begun.

A Question of Paternity

He'd known all along that it was going to be hopeless. From the minute Jane's mother — dignified, in control, her lined face determinedly betraying no trace of her recent grief — had opened the door to welcome him, and across the small space from the living-room where she was standing with her hand indecisively on the knob, Lisa had seen the enormous and expensive teddy bear he was carrying. Her lip had curled in scorn, she'd flung up her sleek dark head like a pony defiantly tossing its mane, and turned her back on him, cut him out, made her decision. And after that, all the week, hardly a word — only those black, furious glares of hostility when he tried to speak to her. There was just no way of getting through. She didn't want to know.

It would have been uncomfortable enough if she'd accepted him. He'd never had even the remotest inkling that an idyllic fortnight with a young and impressionable fellow-tourist in Venice (well, he supposed it must have been idyllic, though he'd been back to Venice many times, and had forgotten that early episode of calf-love for a blushing English rose whose face he couldn't even recall clearly) had produced an off-spring.

He'd never dreamed that he had a daughter, the fruit of his loins, living in blissful anonymity in the depths of the Midlands. In a tiny terraced house that would have fitted snugly into his open-plan flat looking out over Regent's Park. It wasn't possible. There must be some mistake.

But there wasn't any mistake. At least, no mistake he could correct at this stage. By the time he was dazedly facing the solicitor whose painful duty it had been to break the news that the girl's mother — Jane Bradshaw, perhaps he would remember, had been tragically killed in a car accident, and had left her daughter — their daughter — in her father's care, it was too late to start demanding blood tests and applying to contest paternity, or whatever action he might have taken if the wretched woman had been alive. Not — trying to dredge his memory about the fortnight with the blushing English rose — that it was impossible exactly; well, it might have been possible, he had to admit that. A few recollections of silver hair in profusion on a pillow of Venetian moonlight — soft as the glimmer of night on the dreaming water outside their window — good heavens, what on earth was he thinking? Silver hair? Ash blonde, she must have been, then — .

So he'd had to accept this unknown and unwanted daughter being foisted on him by the shade of a dead woman and a certain uncomfortable remembrance of himself when young and in Venice — younger, anyway, since the child was now, unbelievably, thirteen years old. His daughter. Her daughter. Their daughter. And he'd never known. Didn't even want to know when the solicitor suggested that a meeting with the girl might be in order. Now that she'd had a chance to recover somewhat from the shock and grief of her mother's death. She would no doubt be just as apprehensive about her new father as he was about her.

His immediate reaction of withdrawal and the mention of a good girl's boarding school where he could pack the off-spring away and never have to acknowledge her existence except for regular cheques in neat envelopes, met with a pained and incredulous silence. The solicitor — an earnest soul whom Richard thereupon began to hate with all the fury of a person who has organised his life and finds that fate can overturn the best-laid plans of mice and successful photographers of architecture, who do not have to have any contact with humanity unless they choose to seek it — plainly found his attitude utterly lacking in all the finer sensibilities of virtuous existence. The girl, it was pointed out to him again, was his own flesh and blood. Recently bereaved. Surely he must feel it his duty, if nothing else, to visit her — give her what comfort and consolation he could in this dark hour — . Get to know her in the familiar surroundings of her home before (a steepling of the fingers in disapproval here) attempting to uproot her from all that had been loved and dear for her thirteen years of existence. And, trying to cloak his resentment and frustration, Richard had brusquely agreed to the suggestions that were made. Best to get it over with, do his God-damned duty, and escape as quickly as possible.

After the unhappy fiasco of his arrival with the obviously redundant teddy bear which Jane's mother, the elderly Mrs. Bradshaw, whisked away into regions unseen in a generous gesture intended to alleviate hostilities so far as they could be alleviated, he put his foot in it again by enquiring where he should garage his car.

Lisa spoke for the first time, dark eyes smouldering, voice tight with contempt.

"Mummy thought it was all right to leave hers outside. Ours, I mean. Or are you afraid somebody might breathe on yours?"

Sweating, he escaped after a meal that seemed endless, into the room Mrs Bradshaw had ready for her guest, which she said had been her daughter's. Almost, panic set in, a feeling which he had taken care to remain out of reach of for years. It was like going back in time. *Nobody* lived in rooms with crochet chair covers and patchwork quilts and a text on the wall that said: 'God is Love' any more — did they? Still, it was only for a week. Though he was shivering already, there was no central heating in the house, it was damned cold, and he doubted whether there was an electric blanket. A hot-water bottle, more like. Oh, no, he thought, he'd make the arrangements about that good girl's boarding school as soon as he decently could, and forget the whole impossible business.

It was Mrs Bradshaw who, towards the end of that strained and awful week — the longest week Richard had ever spent in his life tentatively mentioned the Fair.

"You'd like to go, love? You always went with your Mum. I'm sure your — Mr Langdon — will take you?" Her gentle eyes pleaded with Lisa's tight, shut face.

Richard — in a surge of relief that there was only one more day to endure before he could get away — practically snarled that certainly he would take Lisa to the Fair. He'd do his duty to the last drop of his blood. And, in the manner of convict and jailor — though it was difficult to decide which was which — he and his daughter set out that evening to cross the allotments to where the lights and laughter of the Fair threw a rainbow of merriment into the peace of the darkening sky, where one star hung lazily.

Teeth clenched, Richard bestrode the gaudily painted carousel horses while tinned music shrieked in his ears. He failed to knock down the coconuts, at which Lisa simply curled her lip. He chomped his way through, a disgusting mess of purple which was called 'Lovers Candy', and nearly broke his capped tooth on a toffee apple. At least, he thought, he had the satisfaction of knowing Lisa was hating every minute as fiercely as he was himself. Judging by her face, anyway.

At the Dodgems, shouldering his way through the crowd, he shoved her unceremoniously into a car marked 'Jet' and climbed into another with the legend 'Rover' in red on the side. He'd no sooner sat down on the uncomfortable seat and twisted the wheel than something hit him. Shook him up, every bone. Surfacing, as though from deep waters he blinked dazedly to see her lining 'Jet' up for a second attack, the tight, shut face no longer tight and shut, but blazing with emotion.

His blood, so sternly suppressed for the last week, seethed. The little — !

That was it, that was enough! She'd asked for what she was going to get! He suffered the second ramming from 'Jet' with no more than a compressing of already compressed lips, turned the wheel and went after her, finding that when he hit her square, knocking her into the side so that her long black hair flew, a shout escaped his lips, unheard in the general din.

Like a fury, she was turning to attack again, but he was ready. Crack! Crunch! This time both of them yelled, vituperation on his lips and hers, eyes alight, fighting to the death. Kill! Kill! Kill!

"I hate you," screamed Lisa, as she scored a hit. "I hate y — eee — ooo — w."

And he could — to his chagrin — think of nothing more original.

"I hate — y — eee — ooo — w."

"I'll kill you," Lisa wept, ramming him from a particularly vicious angle so that he spun and banged his head.

"Girl! Damned — girl!"

He was shaking uncontrollably, blinking through his own tears. She managed to knock the front of the luckless 'Rover' sideways, her face pale now, screwed up with grief and pain, glittering red and green under the lights as she lifted a hand to wipe her eyes.

"It's — not — fair!"

He echoed her shriek with his own, hitting her head on.

"Too damned right, it's not fa — ai — r!"

Not — CRASH! — bloody — TAKE THAT! — fair — !

He could hardly stand, once he got out of the car, his legs were buckling, his head swimming. He felt sick. He held onto the post that propped up the canopy of lights, seeing them switch colours through a dim haze.

Thin arms were around his waist, tentatively.

"Dad?" said a small, frightened voice. "Dad? Are you all right?"

He turned his head thickly.

"There's blood on your face," he got out, fumbling for his handkerchief, heedless of the fine silk. He mopped at her clumsily.

"Dad?" It was hardly more than a

82

whisper. "Dad, I'm sorry."

Somehow he had let go of the post, and the small trembling body was in his arms. Where, he told himself with surprise, that small, trembling body belonged.

"Don't worry," he said, stroking the tangled dark hair — his own black hair, Jane had been blonde, he remembered again, with a quivering of something, some emotion he couldn't have named, into life within him. "Don't cry. Everything's going to be fine now. You'll see."

She was weeping noisily into his shirt, shaking with the violence of her sobs. He held her. Just held her. Wasn't that, he asked himself, what a father was for?

Summing up Leo
(July 24 – Aug 23)

Leo is a bold sign, 'masculine' in the sense of being positive. It represents the 'Yang' of the 'Yin-Yang' duality.

Planet is the Sun, and the warmth and brightness of the sun is reflected in all around it.

Lucky colours: Sun colours, yellow and orange.

Flowers: Sunflower. The laurel crown of victory also belongs to Leo.

Metal: Gold.

Animal: Lion.

Tarot card: Strength — usually depicted as a lion being tamed by a beautiful maiden.

Scent: Olibanum.

Precious stones: Chrysolite and catseye.

Lucky number:1

Lucky day: Sunday

Key concepts: Power, creation, pride.

The mythological story for Leo is that of the Nemean Lion, which could not be captured or killed by usual methods as its skin repelled iron and steel weapons.

Killing the Nemean Lion was one of the Twelve Labours of Hercules, who lost a finger when he fought the beast, after it wounded him in the hand with its teeth.

Positive keynotes: Generous, creative, enthusiastic, organised and organising, tolerant, expansive, theatrical.

Negative trends: Bullying ways, stuck up manners, critical of others' approach, fixed ideas and conversation, conceited and arrogant.

Character: Simple kingship, likes to be seen to lead. Interfering with the harmony of established groups of colleagues or friends. Affectionate with those in the 'in' crowd.

Virgo
(Aug 24 – Sept 23)

SUN in Virgo. Virgo contemplates perfection. Craft(wo)manship serves you: analytical traits bring a discrimination to assume breadth of vision.

Your tolerance vies with self dedication to skim waves of sublime passion and be modest without being self conscious and too puritanical. Although sceptical at first, systematic, impartial optimism leads to emotional interests. Curb fickle and unenthusiastic ways and you could go far.

Enormous creative energies have to be channelled correctly. Usually you will have above average muscular strength and a strong heart.

You are attracted to people in hazardous occupations. You often rush into romantic situations and have a wild passion in affairs. You have a good sense of timing. You can be too forceful and defiant due to your keen sense of justice.

Proper investments and speculations will pay off.

Sun in Virgo. Earth, Mutable, Negative.

Your emblem is the Virgin; also, like Gemini, you are a dualistic sign. These two things, dualism and 'virginity', combine to give you an inherent ambiguity in the following ways: wishing as you do to maintain your natural purity, you seek to avoid 'tainting' by outside influences. Simultaneously you try to prevent the birth — ie expression — of feelings that gestate within.

The former trait can produce isolation; the latter is responsible for your reputation for slowness. These are misapprehensions, though you yourself can tend to perpetuate such misunderstandings. Because, in preserving your spiritual chastity, you can become too private, too removed from others: hence, when you do express your feelings, you release them not without some measure of pain. This is the result of your emotions, in their having accumulated power through retention, being publicly torn from their source.

I have concentrated in my choice of story on the lighter aspect of Virgo and selected IT'S AN ILL WIND, which details an unlikely and highly entertaining meeting that could lead to — well, read it and see for yourself.

The heroine of this diverting encounter possesses the typical duality of Virgo. She has her own standards and is reluctant to lower them, but on the other hand, can adapt to changing circumstances.

It's an Ill Wind

I was sitting in the window-seat at the end of the top corridor in what had formerly been the East Wing when I encountered our new tenant — or rather, he encountered me. Took me by surprise, in fact. I didn't even know he'd arrived, or else I wouldn't have been dreaming there in the winter twilight, seized unaccountably by a mood of exquisite melancholy as I stared unseeing over the blue-shadowed lawns outside the window, the haunting wraiths of snow-laden trees.

The voice snapped me back to the present with a jerk. Smooth, confident, very sure of itself and its power to charm.

"Why, hello there. Are you the ghost of this ancient mansion? A very lovely phantom, if I may say so, Miss — ."

I turned slowly without replying. He was a typical media person, dressed in a manner suitable for the country. Corduroy, a loose — but expensive — sweater, a knotted cravat at his throat. The hair was thick, turning grey, expertly styled. The eyes already assessing my availability and potential. I could almost see his thoughts. It would be so useful to have a woman on tap, as it were, when he decided to withdraw into his rural retreat and fiddle with his recordings, put his notes in order, or whatever it was he intended to do here when he wasn't striding the highly-powered corridors of the Beeb or Elstree Studios or wherever he'd come from. Save a lot of bother, make it just part of the furniture, if there was some female he could whisk out whenever he fancied a candle-lit dinner *a deux* in one of the country inns and a night of romance to follow. What a joke! But I was suddenly roused from my melancholy by an imp of mischief that prompted me to play up to his opening gambit. Why not? What had I got to lose?

"You must be the new tenant of Number 4," I said, allowing a note of sweet confusion at his blatant admiration to colour my voice. I veiled my eyes in the manner of a shrinking violet. "I'm — pleased to meet you."

"Call me Russ," he invited, his glinting gaze suggesting that already there was some sort of spell between us. This thing is bigger than both of us, darling, why should we try to fight it?

"I'm Elizabeth," I offered huskily, watching with interest as he assumed the air of a man who has already conquered. He leaned over, took my hand gallantly, and kissed the tips of my fingers, murmuring:

"Then hello, Elizabeth. Look — er — why don't you come in for a drink? We can't talk here in the corridor."

His eyes had by now scanned my hand, he'd satisfied himself that I wasn't wearing a ring on my wedding finger, and I helped to foster the illusion of a girl on her own who had been bowled over by his fatal charm with a casual shrug and an intimate:

"Why not? I'm a free agent."

A grasp beneath my elbow propelled the unsuspecting fly into the spider's kitchen — in other words, Flat Number 4. Through the entrance hall carpeted in blue into a sitting room that looked like it had been specially designed as a background for this slightly ageing Romeo to seduce any Juliets who wandered in out of the cold. Warm, reassuring, comfortable, with the track practically signposted into the adjoining bedroom. I sank into the clutches of a Habitat suite of immense proportions, and watched with a limpid gaze as he made for the drinks trolley.

"What would you like?"

"Oh, just a fruit juice, please. I have to watch my figure."

"It's more fun," he said with a conspiratorial gleam. "If you let someone else do the watching. Yours is most definitely a figure worth looking at, darling. It must have been fate that brought me to this flat, brought us together. You live here?"

I nodded, setting the drink he handed me carefully down on a polished table.

"And what do you do?" he queried, lifting a hand before I could answer. "No, don't tell me! You're an actress who gave up the bright lights because she wanted to be alone. Or a writer of best sellers who prefers to keep out of the public eye."

"Actually," I said. "I do research work. I'm connected with an outfit that specialises in the paranormal."

He was only half listening. The other half was busy weighing up the cleavage revealed by my black dress.

"The paranormal, eh? Ghosties and ghouls and things that go bump in the night?"

"No, genuine hauntings," I said, twisting the glass with the fruit juice in between my fingers.

He laughed in a would-be-tolerant manner.

"Are there such things?"

"Oh, definitely. This house is haunted, for instance."

"Come on, my love," quoth Russ, raising his brows amusedly. "Are you trying to frighten me away?" His tone was playful.

"Not at all," I said. "I thought you might be interested."

He slid onto the Habitat couch beside me with the ease born of long practise, and wound a tentacle round my shoulders.

"At the moment, I'm only interested in you, darling. You can haunt me any time you like."

"I take my work seriously," I snapped, shrugging his groping hand away, and he prepared to humour me. After all, the evening was as yet but young, I could see him calculating.

"Tell me about the ghost."

"There are several here. A Headless Lady — she was executed in the reign of Mary Tudor — and a Black Monk — "

"What's a Black Monk got to do with the house?"

"He doesn't have anything to do with

it," I said. "He just came here when his monastery was destroyed and a multi-storey car-park was built on the site later. This is a good place for ghosts, an old Elizabethan mansion, all the little nooks and corners, wainscoting, mullioned windows. They have to have the right atmosphere to be able to haunt properly. The Black Monk couldn't have coped with a multi-storey car-park."

I could tell that this ardent would-be-lover-boy didn't believe a word I was saying. He'd already decided I was all body and no brain. Annoyed, I extracted myself from the depths of the couch and said briskly:

"Come with me."

"Where to?" That had him off balance.

"I'll show you a haunting."

The landing at the top of the servants' stairs (now referred to as the Fire Exit) had all the right ingredients. Dimly lit, with the staircase leading down to a cavernous hall from which the back door opened. On this winter evening, hushed and expectant.

I paused at the top with my hand on the bannisters.

"Do you feel how cold it is?" I whispered, but the amorous Russ wasn't having any of the flannel. His arm came round me from behind, lingering outrageously on my bosom.

"Don't worry, darling, I can warm you up."

"You admit it *is* cold though?"

"Probably the central heating. I'll speak to the caretaker about it," he said, beginning to go into some heavy breathing.

I shrugged him off once again.

"Just stand there and wait."

"What for?"

"You'll see."

Somewhat wearily, he stood. I concentrated, staring down into the hall below. Out of the shadows, a shape began to emerge, take on form. A full-skirted gown, the glimmer of white neck, horrifyingly slashed into bloody nothingness. Like a wraith, the Headless Lady drifted across the hall at the foot of the stairs, lingered, then disappeared into the wall beyond. I waited until she had gone, then turned triumphantly.

"Did you see her?"

Russ's eyes were glazed with lust.

"My God, Elizabeth, in that black dress, with the light shining on your hair, you look like Carole Lombard waiting for Clark Gable to sweep her off into a clinch. I could go for you in a big way, you know that?"

"But did you *see* her?" I was getting exasperated.

"I was looking at you, my love. Talk about sex goddesses — you knock them all for six. I could do a lot for you, maybe it's time to revive the Vamp image — I'll have a word with Melchett about it — he could get you an audition, you could do a test — ."

"Did you see her?" I interrupted coldly, unimpressed by his wild enthusiasm to launch me in pictures.

With difficulty, he dragged his eyes from the curve of my breast, and clenched his hands, hardly able to wait.

"Who?"

I gave up.

"Never mind. Look, you go back, I'll be with you in a minute."

"Where are you going?" he demanded suspiciously.

I leaned across and flicked his nose with my finger.

"Just back to my place for a few little things I might need for the night."

He gave a sort of gasp.

"You're driving me crazy," he moaned thickly.

I kissed my hand and transferred the kiss to his slobbering lips.

"Baby," I breathed huskily. "You've seen nothing yet."

After he'd gone, scuttling away, I thought, to down his drink in bewilderment at his own good fortune as he tremblingly waited for the fun to start, I hesitated a moment at the top of the stairs, the melancholy mood sweeping over me once more. Then I roused myself and walked down the stairs and through the wall to join the rest of the team in our little metaphysical corner of time.

"It was a good try, Elizabeth," said the Black Monk sympathetically.

"I did my best," the Headless Lady assured me in her wispy disembodied voice.

"I know. You were great. It wasn't

your fault," I said. I was reflecting as I had been earlier on, before the amorous Russ appeared on the scene, that when people wouldn't even take the traditional forms of haunting, what chance was there for a Thirties ghost with blonde hair and a dress that might have come from a second-hand clothes shop? I wasn't exactly getting a lot of job satisfaction. Maybe it was time for a change.

I thought about the Vamp image — the audition Russ had promised — the test — .

"What would you say," I asked the rest of the team consideringly, "if I told you I was contemplating a new career in films?"

Summing up Virgo
(August 24 – Sept 23)

Element: Earth.
Birthstone: Carnelian.
Planet: Mercury.
Colour: Blue.
Number: 5.
Herb: Fennel.

Parts of the body ruled by Virgo: The intestines.

Keynotes: Dependability, conscientiousness, practicality, modesty, humanity.

Lucky plants: Narcissis, vervain.

Lucky colours: Narcissis colours, yellow-green, cream and pale brown.

Scent: Narcissis.

Metal: Mercury.

Tarot card: Temperance.

Animals: Bat, mink.

Lucky gems: Peridot, agate, opal.

Typical Virgos have a very good mind and — via the ruling planet, Mercury — an interest in and ability in acquiring and amassing information and in communications. They have a flair for seemingly unimportant detail which will turn out to be of basic importance in the end.

Virgos are not necessarily virgins — in fact in astrology, the sign of the Virgin indicates fertility as well as self-improvement. Virgos may have a hidden streak of deep and passionate sexuality which could lie hidden for literally years — until the right person comes on the scene!

Libra
(Sept 24 – Oct 23)

SUN in Libra subjects attain harmony. They aspire to a trinity of beauty, justice and idealism. You have the ability to adjust circumstances and to compare once place to another. Your particular brand of diplomacy may be described as waiting for the chance to move in for the kill.

You can be helpful but sometimes a little interfering. Your friendliness is sometimes dependent on suitable partners and victims for charms. Although you appear to be wavering and easily influenced, firmness will add consistence to decisive victories in contentious areas. You may appear lazy but you are not as dependent and easily influenced as you appear. Sometimes you are a mirror for the insincerity of others.

Sun in Libra. Air, Cardinal, Positive.

A fascination for people — as the reflections of your own image — can lead you to luxuriate in the company of others. For better or worse, you are frequently motivated by the desire for universal applause — or popularity — sometimes becoming provocative when the desired acclaim is not forthcoming. The reason you become provocative is because, if it were at all possible, you would actually force your detractors to like you.

Possessing a great capacity for both physical and intellectual games, you will often pursue issues even to the extent of amplifying them into moral crusades. The converse of this is your tendency towards impartiality, allowing issues to settle into a state of artificial neutrality in order to satisfy an instinctive need for equilibrium.

Yours is the only sign whose emblem is an inanimate object — the Balances — though you are indeed a sign which is thoroughly human.

⋆ ⋆ ⋆

CHOICE OF WEAPONS was written especially for this book, to illustrate

Libra, and in my view does so admirably, partly because Dilys Gater has captured the illusiveness of what 'balance' is all about.

There is no real ending here, for the hero (or anti-hero's) apparent loss of his prey and the failure of his own weapons of riches and money to match others of beauty, youth and intangibility which he cannot comprehend, may be only a setback.

Perhaps, as the scales sway, his prey will return to him and he will be able to pursue his seige and emerge victorious. Or will he? He does indeed see everyone else as a reflection of himself, but we feel he has no idea of what Lyssa is really like, nor what she thinks. Perhaps we do not even know that ourselves. Anything could happen here, in the timeless moment when the scales are balanced before they fall.

Choice of Weapons

Bik had planned every move with the greatest of care. There was no way he could fail, really. He had all the weapons he needed, he had amassed them over a long period of time. And now they would stand him in good stead. He knew this was what he had been waiting for, what it had all been about.

Lyssa was a dream, simply a dream. Unbelievable. She was twenty-two, with a shape that suggested all sorts of X-certificate things to a man like Bik, and hair down to her waist, naturally blond, the colour of warm sand. What was more, she was a lady. A real lady, not one of your tarted-up types, the sort he was used to. Her eyes were innocent and clear, and when he listened to her voice he could feel the years falling from him like back-packs, the future beckoning again with illusory promise of renewed youth.

When he first saw her, he knew he had to have her. When he spoke to her, met her candid gaze, he realised immediately that it would have to be on the only terms she would find acceptable. No hotel rooms, no discreet flat where he could set her up at his convenience. No, there was nothing else for it — he would have to marry her.

His first reaction was relief that he was still free, he had no missus hanging round his neck to be got rid of, no 'ex's' to make trouble. He had managed to dodge 'the tender trap' all his life, scarper before anyone could hook him. He had been proud of that, when all his mates gloomed into their beer about their problems.

Now, though, he realised that he had never really understood what it was all about. If only Lyssa would promise to marry him, he would go down on his knees and sob with relief — well, in a manner of speaking. If she refused him, that was where the trouble lay. He went cold at the thought. Never. He simply could not let her slip through his fingers, not now he had found her. He would never come across another girl like Lyssa in his life again. He had to hold her and keep her.

So this morning he was ready to lead up to his proposal. He had the ring in his pocket, a twenty-grand solitaire. And he had the day to persuade her to accept it.

They had driven from London yesterday,

arriving last night and booking into the hotel late. Lyssa had said she was tired. She did, he realised with concern, look a bit pale and peaky. She gave him her lovely smile as she left him in the bar and went up to 'my beauty sleep and an early night, all ready for the big adventure tomorrow.'

Into the wilderness, he had told her proudly. He'd take her into the mountains, far away from it all, just nature all around. She ruffled his hair, laughed and said gently:

"You are such a romantic little boy still, aren't you? In spite of everything. Well, if you want to be Robin Hood and take me to the forest, I'll unpack my Maid Marion gown and hood."

And here she was, running lightly down the stairs to breakfast, like one of those flowers — daffs, he thought — all dancing green and yellow in a willowy thing that clung to her lissom body (steady on, Bik, this isn't that sort of holiday, he told himself rather regretfully, as he tried to keep his mind on higher things) and her hair sliding over her shoulders bright as melted butter.

He started the campaign over her orange juice and cereal (full English breakfast for himself). His business deals, stocks and shares, bonds, the Euro-connection, the Argentine (be vague about that, don't give too much away). She was impressed, he could tell, and his spirits began to soar.

"How much do you think the old banger outside cost me?" he pursued more confidently.

Her smile dazzled him like a spring morning.

"I don't know. It's a lovely colour. A lot, I suppose. Thousands?"

It took the rest of the breakfast, and the coffee and two cigarettes before he had finished detailing the specifications and how much each extra item had set him back, but it was worth it to see her breathless interest. She had her eyes very wide, almost as though she couldn't take in what he was saying.

As he drove off down the drive, heading for the 'wilderness', he started to tell her about the property. Well, properties. He took them each in turn, and was amused that she knew so little about the market.

Even the difference between the relative values of Belgravia and Notting Hill Gate seemed to have passed over her glossy head.

"I've never taken much interest in Daddy's property," she confessed as they stopped for morning coffee at a quaint Coffee Shoppe in the middle of nowhere, where they had to push through some sheep to reach the door. "I won't have to worry about inheriting it, everything goes to Simon. I really am more interested in the simple things of life."

The trouble was, Bik had heard that line so many times before from peroxided gold-diggers — but he pushed this unworthy comparison away immediately. Lyssa was different. She just did not understand that there were some women who were as devious as cork-screws. He patted her hand where it lay on the snowy cloth indulgently, and proceeded to explain, including the difference made by percentages of interest, simple and compound, just how glittering his possessions in the property line happened to be. Lyssa smiled politely, but suggested they could talk while he drove, she really would like to see the historic castle he had mentioned.

Before they reached the castle, he had covered his overseas properties and some of his investments in art and other moveables.

"I never buy or wear anything that isn't the very best," he declared, as she pointed breathlessly to the rugged tower, ivy-clad, that was visible above the tangled woods and greenery around them. "Yes, that's it. For instance, did you notice my watch? Here, have a look. Cartier. And my shoes. Gucci. And — ."

But he had to stop to negotiate the narrow entrance gate that led to the castle, and something about the place touched his soul, prompting him that perhaps she had heard enough, perhaps now was the time to get out the jeweller's box.

For the castle was small, romantic in the extreme, and in the soft dream-like sun-lit setting the air was still, the grass and flowers like something from legend, the world very far away. Birds were calling in the surrounding woods. It was still. They were almost alone.

He locked the car and came round to where she stood, staring at the grey stone-work.

Something prompted him, and he cleared his throat.

"It's still owned by a descendant of the family that built it. Lived in, part anyway. We can go in — but first there's something I want to give you."

He put the jeweller's box, unopened, in her hand. She looked up slowly into his face, then her gaze was distracted.

"Oh, oh, how beautiful how gloriously beautiful," she cried, pushing the box carelessly back at him, and running across the grass. A peacock, crowned and regal, was spreading its tail and walking under an ancient tree. A young man was standing with hands on hips, teasing it. He was fair and shabbily dressed, but Bik, watching the scene, saw with a sinking heart that the same something hung about them all, Lyssa, the young man and the bird.

"Oh, how beautiful, how beautiful," Lyssa said again, transfigured. But she was not looking at the peacock.

Summing up Libra
(Sept 23 – Oct 23)

Lucky day: Friday.
Lucky gems: Jade, emerald, turquoise.
Planet: Venus.
Colour: Green.
Metal: Copper.
Tarot card: Justice (scales).
Perfumes: Rose, sandalwood.
Incense: Patchouli oil, rose.
Creatures: Sparrow, swan, lynx.
Deities: Aphrodite, Venus, Rhiannon.
Tree: Myrtle.
Herbs: Sorrel, redcurrant.
Manner: Kind, understanding, warm, affectionate.

The legend for Libra is that of the scales used to weigh the souls of the dead in Ancient Egyptian belief of the afterlife. Good and bad deeds done by the dead soul were weighed in the balance to see how the soul should be judged.

Scorpio
(Oct 24 – Nov 22)

SCORPIO 'the Scorpion' is a much maligned sign as it is often trying to prepare for the worst. To show the complex nature of Scorpio I have included details of attendant planets that real Scorpios may or may not have in their makeup.

Sometimes Scorpios sting themselves fearing a situation to be worse than it is, or out of sheer bile. This story sums up the popular picture of a typical Scorpio:

A Scorpion once tried to cross a stream using a frog as a ferry. It assured the frog it would let him go without hurting him on the other side. But half way across, the fretful frog felt a sting. "Now we will both drown," he said. "Why did you do that?" The Scorpion's reply was: "I felt like it!"

Sun in Scorpio. Scorpio probes deeply to obtain satisfaction. For you, excessive control is a way to eliminate enemies.

111

You are intense and fanatical. You have exceptionally strong recuperative faculties which have the ability to destroy all obstacles. You do, however, have a reserved, suspicious and resentful nature which may not engender forgiveness nor help you in your aspirations.

Energy comes from reserved and secretive passions through planning followed through in a jealous though courageous manner.

Mercury in Scorpio. You have an insight into the needs of others and have the ability to manipulate the financial resources of institutions. You use tact and discretion to unveil the fears of other people. You enable them to discuss taboo subjects such as sexuality and death.

You are likely to receive some form of legacy later in life. You are most highly respected for intensity and dedication.

Moon in Scorpio. Fixed Water (lunar).

This is seen by astrologers as one of the most difficult placements. It gives exceptionally strong emotions and highly developed sensitivity bordering on the psychic. Because of deep fear of abandonment it is your greatest challenge to find someone you can trust. With perception and understanding of human nature you are painfully aware of the problems and foibles of others. You refuse to admit that you yourself are only human and will sublimate feelings into a challenging career or more negatively, drink and drugs.

It may be the case that you had a traumatic childhood, the wounds from which rarely, if ever, heal. Your personal challenge is to let go of personal memories: look positively towards the future, realising that whatever you have suffered is only part of life's learning process.

Sun in Scorpio. Water, Fixed, Negative.

You can be very self-protective and, being so, can sometimes over-promote your own cause. You can rightly or wrongly be accused at times of excess. Yet much of your activity is really a ploy to stop you from showing your feelings to just anybody, as that would be considered by you as exposing, not your strength but your vulnerability. You don't like to be too open, showing others what a marshmallow you really are at heart.

113

Therefore you have a tendency to affect a worldliness and repress your feelings, which you try to reserve specifically for occasions of import. Herein originates your reputation for intenseness.

★ ★ ★

I have deliberately selected a humorous story for Scorpio. CIRCLE OF FEAR is amusing but illustrates very well the fear of this sign to prepare for and anticipate the worst. So often, as in this case, the worst may never happen, but the motto of the true Scorpio it might well be that of the Scouts in that they constantly feel the need to 'Be Prepared!'

A Circle of Fear

'Smiler' Smith lowered his bulky frame wearily into a chair, his eyes on the black bag beside him on the table. What had made him do it? He'd kept clean since he came out of jail three years ago, thought the past was behind him. He'd married Marie, and settled down to a law-abiding, if uneventful life as a dock-side labourer.

He sighed gustily. Well, the deed was done now. There was no going back, and anyway, some of the stuff was good.

He drew the bag towards him and pulled out a handful of objects that glittered under the unshaded bulb of the shabby room. A flash of brilliant crimson drew his eyes to a large and elaborately jewelled golden ring amid the clutter, and he lifted it out to examine it more closely.

A huge ruby was set in the centre, like a fantastic red eye, and around it were clustered other stones formed into strange shapes 'Smiler' didn't recognise. But its gaudiness appealed to his taste. He slipped it onto his little finger, pushing it over the thick knuckle, and held it up to admire it, turning it this way and that.

A sound behind him made him turn his head sharply. Marie was standing in the doorway that led to their bedroom, her black hair streaming over her nightdress, rubbing the sleep from her eyes. She saw the ring, and stiffened.

"Where d'you get that? What you been doing, Smiler?"

He looked at her guiltily, and she sank into the opposite chair, her face going white.

"Smiler, you haven't gone and — ? After keeping straight all this time?"

"Well, I'm sorry love. I don't know what made me do it. But nobody saw me — ."

"Where did you pinch the stuff from?" Marie asked resignedly.

"That Professor Something-or-other. Archaeology bloke, big house at Hampstead," 'Smiler' said, watching her. "Look, love, I really am sorry. I won't do it again, honest to God. But it's done now, and I can't put the stuff back, can I?"

"You don't have to wear it, though," Marie flashed at him, looking at the ring with distaste.

'Smiler' closed his hand up as though to protect it. "I was only trying it on", he growled. "Worth a mint, this ring is. Come from one of them Pharaoh's tombs, I shouldn't wonder."

"Let me look," Marie said, and her

116

voice shook suddenly. She stared at it, then thrust his hand away. "Take it off, Smiler. Throw it away. Throw all the stuff away."

"Now hang on, love — "

"It's cursed, that's what it is. I've heard of them cursed rings from the Egyptian tombs. Throw it away, Smiler." She put her hands on his shoulders, and looked up into his face. "Please. For me."

"Well, all right love, if it means that much to you," the burly man said gruffly, tugging at the ring. But it would not move from his finger. They tried soap, cream and every way they could think of to remove the ring, until 'Smiler's' finger was raw and aching, but the more they tried, the tighter it became.

"It's the curse, that's what it is," Marie kept saying hysterically.

"All right, love. Calm down. Look, I'll go and have it cut away tomorrow. First thing. Okay? Now, for pity's sake, let's get some sleep."

But it seemed that peaceful sleep was not for the wicked. 'Smiler' awoke in the dawn, trembling and sweating from the

117

horrors of the dark tombs and glassy-eyed idols pronouncing curses, that had haunted his dreams. He paced up and down the room, tugging occasionally at the ring and swearing at it, until the alarm went off and Marie got up.

They had breakfast, then 'Smiler' stood up, saying purposefully, "I'm going straight to have this — ." He paused, having glanced automatically out of the window at the sound of a car drawing up outside. "Oh, no!"

"What's up?" Marie asked.

"It's old Carman. He's outside — ."

"Police? Oh, Smiler." Marie sank back into her chair. She heaved a huge sigh, and shook her head resignedly.

"But what put them onto me?" the burly man growled, clenching his fists. "I never made no mistake, I know I didn't. I could say I never went near the place, and they'd never prove that I did."

"With that ring on your finger? Don't make me laugh," Marie said caustically, and 'Smiler' looked slowly down at his hand.

"Oh, yes. The curse — ," he growled.

The C.I.D. man who knocked on the

door of their flat was slightly startled at his reception. He had called to ask if 'Smiler' could give him any information about a certain Johnny Decco, who had been his friend in the old days, not to arrest him. But the big man held out his wrists.

"Okay, I admit it. I'll come quietly. But for pity's sake get this blasted ring off my finger."

He felt, as the ring was sawn away, as though a load was being lifted from him. Though in police custody, at least he would be free of the dreadful curse.

The ring slipped from his hand. 'Smiler' stared for a moment, then grabbed it to look closer, an awful suspicion coming to him. Then he threw it down, and opened his mouth to roar.

For his finger was banded with green, and the 'gold' ring was stamped on the-inside, 'Made in Birmingham'.

Summing up Scorpio

Lucky gem: Citrine.
Planet: Pluto.

119

Element: Water.
Colour: Red.
Lucky number: 9.
Plant: Basil.
Lucky gem: Turquoise, ruby.
Metal: Iron, steel.
Tarot card: Death (renewal).
Animal: Wolf.
Scorpio rules: The sex organs.
Key words: 'I desire'.
Characteristics: Dedicated, magnetic, passionate, sensual, aware.
Negative: Resentful, secretive,
Life meditation: .

Bulldozing rubble and problems into a ditch in your mind, then imagining you are planting seeds and watching them flower.

Taurus and Scorpio form a see-saw, going up and down in turn. Try to imagine you are sitting on one end of the see-saw and allow yourself to fly up and leave problems behind.

The higher consciousness symbol of Scorpio is the phoenix — the bird that rises from the ashes. Try to rise above your problems or anything in your life that is holding you down.

Sagittarius
(Nov 23 – Dec 21)

SUN in Sagittarius. You have a great capacity for happiness and can have a deep belief that things will get better if you work and make efforts to overcome obstacles.

This sign is connected with the functioning of the brain and relates to the higher mind. Your aspirations are linked to your ideals. Long journeys are planned and undertaken with care. Outdoor life can add to your enjoyment of simple pleasures.

Sagittarius claims that wisdom gives a true perspective. You explore and explain. Your subtle moves increase your intuitive powers and the ability to prophesy. In this way you are able to establish connections while still conserving your ambitions.

You are honest to the point of bluntness. Your impulsive, flighty actions are made worse by objectionable behaviour from others. Impulses happen and are often lucky, but you can be careless with winnings. No matter how bad situations are you are optimistic that there will be an improvement ahead soon.

You have a jovial nature which others may find too bold, blunt and improvised. You are exceptionally versatile and others may see this quality as superficial flightiness.

Sun in Sagittarius. Fire, Mutable, Positive. Yours is the last Fire Sign of the zodiac, after Aries and Leo. The element of Fire, therefore 'grows up' in Sagittarius. The astrological significance of Fire is its power to project the qualities of Spirit.

Such qualities are often seen by you as having a primary, and collective, importance; you see 'spirituality' as being the birthright of mankind. A spiritual awareness is, after all, a great responsibility, and an involvement with it can create depression and/or flippancy, depending on how far you have gone.

Like your opposite sign, Gemini, the dynamics of psychology are very active in Sagittarius. The mixture of Mind and Spirit could therefore, perhaps, suggest to an observer that you have been, so to speak, 'touched by God'. This inspiration, or gift, can swing either way: both religious leadership and idiocy are often considered in their own way as being differing styles of the divine.

★ ★ ★

The story I have chosen to represent Sagittarius is THE SHOT. This is interesting because it illustrates just how the Sagittarian sense of 'divine right' and a conviction of controlling circumstances can be both correct and yet as in this case, result in tragedy.

Sagittarius will take risks — in this case with destiny. He will push life to its limits and brave whatever the consequences are.

But mainly I have included this story because, apart from its sense of destiny and inescapable fate, which no amount of striving can overcome, this is a 'story' in the traditional old-fashioned sense.

The Shot

His mother had had tears in her violet-blue eyes when she told him about his father's death. It was some time after the event, for when his father had died in action in the trenches, Raoul had been only two, his mother forced by circumstances to leave their estate quickly, everything sold to pay the enormous debts. France was crippled by the war. The cost in lives outweighed the millions of francs — and for Raoul and his mother, things were changed for ever.

He was ten by the time she was able to tell him about the curse. They were sitting breakfasting in the small room at the top of the tall house in the Fauberg St Honoré that was all he remembered as 'home'. Their rooms were rented. All their wealth had gone. He was an earnest 'élève' with untidy black hair that persisted in falling down over his forehead. She was a still-slender, still lovely woman who earned her living in one of the big Paris fashion houses, selling gowns to women who were not half so beautiful. And Raoul's father?

"It was his father, your grand-père," his mother told him, lifting her coffee-cup. "He too was a dealer in old and beautiful things. It was at a remote chateau, and he saw the Archer and knew he had to have it. Not to sell, you understand, but for himself. So he attempted to buy it. But the owner of the chateau refused to sell. He said the Archer had been brought from Greece by an earlier member of his family, secretly and with violence. An old Greek woman had stopped the donkey-cart as they were hurrying with the statue to the sea, and cursed it and him. The Archer, she said, would obtain his revenge for generations to come. Each person down the male line would die from a shot."

"An arrow?" Raoul queried. He had no sense of humour and never understood subtlety. He was at ease with only two things, facts and money, and so was destined to become immensely successful financially, so that the wealth he accumulated was far greater than the fortune his father had lost.

Maman shrugged delicately.

"Who can tell? But the owner of the chateau vowed that the curse had already taken two members of his family, and he was reluctant to pass such a terrible destiny on. But your grand-père took no notice. He must have the Archer. He brought it home and set it in the place of honour."

"And?"

"Five months later, he was dead. It was a cartridge that killed him, the sort used for hunting foxes. No-one knew who fired the shot."

Even at the age of ten, Raoul had incredible control of his reactions.

"But it was a shot."

"Yes," Maman sighed. "It was a shot."

There was a short pause, while the sun seemed to move interminably slowly across the Paris sky, in contrast to the babble of quicksilver noise and movement that rose from the street below. Then Raoul said:

"And — Papa?"

She gave a tiny Gallic shrug.

"It was in the trenches. A bullet through the lung, and then pneumonia."

"Another shot," said Raoul.

His mother was silent. He glanced across the room to where the Archer stood in the inmost shadowed corner. To the uninitiated, it was a statue of dark stone, with a broken bow. To anyone who had a sixth sense for such things, it was beyond price.

"I will keep it always," he said. "I will never sell it, but it will bring me luck. Don't worry, Maman. No gun ever made will be able to kill me."

"No," she said slowly. "I had a dream two nights ago. The Archer carries for you the curse of Midas. All you touch will turn to gold, Raoul, and you will starve because you cannot eat gold."

He often said afterwards that such a prophesy could not be so. Curses have their own laws, he declared. Unless the curse is a general one, it does not change to suit circumstances. The Archer killed with a shot. His success, his fortune, his business acumen had nothing to do with guns and arrows. Midas, so far as he understood the legend, had never had any dealings with guns or arrows. His mother had probably eaten cheese before retiring and confused a vision of the success ahead of him with a gypsy's warning of doom. No-one could starve because they possessed too much gold. It was not logical.

Until this moment, when, standing in

the Painted Gallery of his own chateau, a glass of Venetian crystal in his hand, the glitter of jewels and beauty on every side, music and perfume from the flowers intoxicating his brain, he looked at the woman who stood beside his youngest son in her white satin bridal gown, lilies of the valley a simple crown for her sleek dark hair. He looked across an unbridgeable chasm of forty years, of the blaze of love in her eyes when they rested upon the man whose hand she clasped, of the thin glittering band on her left hand — and most hurtful of all, her quick glance across to him, Raoul, and a small, secret wave, a little airy kiss blown like thistledown towards him, before she turned away again.

He could feel the arrow as though it was a physical thing. His mother had been right — he had nothing but gold, yet he was starving to death. But the Archer had remained true to the curse too. This time, though, he had not fired the shot himself, he had sent another archer, the tiny Cupid, to bring about Raoul's end. At the instant Raoul set eyes on his youngest son's bride-to-be and smiled at her and greeted her with a courteous "Enchanté, ma'mselle", the golden arrow had pierced his heart. Little by little, even while the wine flowed and the music played and the chatter of the wedding guests rose and fell, Raoul could feel his life blood ebbing away in the most exquisite agony.

He looked across at the Archer, which stood in a place of honour, discreetly spot-lit, at the end of the Gallery. He was not imagining it. The dark stone lips were parted in triumph.

Summing up Sagittarius (Nov 23 – Dec 21)

Flowers, herbs and food:
Dandelion seeds and flower.
Lemon balm — used for weak stomach and debility.
Allspice.
Asparagus, tomatoes, leeks, onions.
Trees: Birch, lime, mulberry, ash, chestnut.
Lucky gems: Topaz, native tin linked to:

Ruling planet: Jupiter.
Country: Spain.
Animals: Hunting dogs, deer, horses, stag.
Vehicle: Motorbike.
Lucky colours: Blue, purple, white.
Lucky number: 9
Lucky day: Thursday
Features: Wild wavy hair, firm posture, head held high. Men are more likely to have beards than other signs. Thick set body in boys. Long legs.
Games: Basketball, archery, dancing.
Style: Eternal student dress.
Likes to dress well and formally.
Fond of polo neck sweaters.
Loose clothing.
Mythic symbol: The centaur, whose unnatural body was at odds with its mind and spirit.
The eternal optimist.

Capricorn
(Dec 22 – Jan 20)

S UN in Capricorn. You will try to do everything with the utmost integrity. You have a strong sense of reverence and a dutiful nature. You are conservative in the extreme, and will always defend the status quo.

You may be compared with your symbol, the goat, climbing the mountain; slowly but surely achieving power and control. You may appear a 'father figure' in a rather strict, austere way. You are highly organised and can be severe.

You are extremely economical and work hard for everything you get. You are very dependable. To others you might appear snobbish and time serving, but they will come to realise that this is only one aspect of your nature. There is a good deal of material expression in your sign: that is, you see upward social mobility and a corresponding degree of riches going hand in hand.

'Aspiration' could well be the watchword for Capricorn and as we have already seen, your emblem, the Mountain Goat, symbolises this characteristic. The animal's function is to ascend any incline until it reaches the summit. Thus you, like your emblem, see the direction of life's path as always being upward, and the more you ascend the incline, the more you outwardly show evidence of your length of journey. To put it very simply, the older and more experienced you get in life, the more you consider you should rightfully have to show for it.

The final rewards are wealth, recognition and status. You therefore have an innate understanding of age as the product of time, though you can make the forgivable mistake of confusing this with the falsehood that physical maturity is synonymous with maturity of the spirit.

I have selected a story called GROWING PAINS to illustrate the attributes of Capricorn. The heroine seems to sum up all the aspirations and strivings as well as the reverential attitude to her hero, that anyone could ask for. She tries everything — or very nearly everything!

On the surface, Capricorn woman is every inch the 'lady' and never reveals her inner turmoil. We feel that Becky goes to great lengths to keep up the right appearance, unaware that her true self is so much more lovely and interesting. But fortunately she has a hero who is worthy of her and there is a magical ending to this bewitching tale, which reflects the romantic yearning within the heart of every Capricorn.

Growing Pains

It was the summer of '58. The last summer of her childhood. The first summer of the woman. She was sixteen that year. Far from engaged, secretly, like her friend Marlene, who ostentatiously hid her cheap silver ring, given to her by Graham, of the Fish Shop, whenever anyone who might notice was about. Becky was not even 'going steady'. In fact, she was not going at all.

She wished, desperately, that she knew what was wrong with her; and/or, alternatively, what it was that she was doing wrong. She must be going off the rails somewhere, because even Betty with the blotches and spots, and Maureen who had ballooned into monstrous puppy-fat, had found themselves 'steadies'. The fact that Becky would not have wanted the thick-lipped (brain-damaged?) Pottle brothers was beside the point. She would have given her soul to be in the position to say 'no' to them.

And there was more to it than the fact that she was always such an embarrassing outsider when the others paired off. Not even the Pottle brothers, not even Graham from the Fish Shop, had wanted her. What was so wrong with her that no single eligible boy in the village ever chose her for a partner at the village 'Hop'? or asked to walk her home? Or wanted to take her out?

By the summer of '58, Becky had reached the point of no return. If she did not find herself a young man before the leaves turned and fell at the turn of the year, she vowed to herself that she would throw herself over the edge of the Quarry; or go out at dawn and hang herself in the woods; or drown herself in the millrace five miles away. Or something. She read Swinburne and Shelley lying on her bed in her little room with the crooked floor and window that rattled in a draught, looking out at the soft ochres and greens and fawns of the countryside beyond her eyrie at the top of the house, the patchwork of distant fields, in a mist of destiny.

But as the summer days began to lengthen and the sky took on that pure cobalt and marguerite, overlaid with gold, of the Duc du Berry's *Book of Hours* with its mediaeval richness, Becky found out why fate had been keeping her apart, untainted. For that was the summer when Gareth Llywellyn and his parents came to live in the gracious house that stood outside the village. And the minute Becky set eyes on Gareth, she was lost.

It did not help matters that all the other girls were lost as well, and Graham and the Pottle brothers and Simon and Geoffrey and Peter Yard who had not managed to grow past four feet ten even though he was sixteen, found themselves cast into outer darkness. They did not possess Gareth's lean, dark Celtic looks,

135

his finely sculptured cheek-bones and thick ebony hair and eyes blue as the lakes of his native Wales at high summer. They did not possess a voice with a lilt that made each deep word sound like music — like the bells of Cantre'r Gwaelor, Becky thought, sounding out by enchantment from the drowned city under the sea. (She had been busy since Gareth had arrived in the village and had read two books on Welsh legends as well as one about the history of the North Wales coal-fields so that she would be able to impress this god if fortune ever presented her with the opportunity to speak to him).

She was more than ever conscious of being poised between 'twelve and twenty' as the people who knew about such things sometimes put it. At the 'difficult age'. What they called the 'teens'. She did not, if she was honest, really know where she was going, though she hoped she would please her mother and pass her exams. They were behind her now, just a memory of the breaking-up of the school term for the holidays, but the results would not be announced for two more months. Her mother asked her for so little. Sometimes she seemed so vague and transparent she was barely there, but Becky knew scholastic success would please her, for it would mean Becky was better equipped to make her own way in the world, and her mother would be able to loosen still further her precarious grasp on reality. Ever since her father had died when she was eleven, of the injuries he had received in the War, Becky's mother had died a little more within herself each day, her spirit gone, fled with him.

Though she was aware that she was the child of a great love, a passion that had eaten up the two it embraced and transcended death, Becky did not feel she could burden her mother by asking for advice when it came to practicalities like hair styles and make-up. Her mother had never, to her knowledge, ever so much as picked up a lip-stick, and her only beauty treatment, which she had practised unswervingly throughout her life, was to brush her long hair a hundred strokes a day before winding it into its knot at the nape of her neck, and to wash her face morning and evening in mild soap and tepid water. The fact that her hair was like molten silver, the finest flaxen blonde, and that her face had the freshness and delicacy of seventeen, seemed to have been some sort of bonus which could not be accounted for. Becky was well aware that she herself had ordinary skin which could erupt embarrassingly into spots on occasion, and that her hair, though long enough to be worn in the fashion as a 'pony-tail', was thick and unruly, as well as being neither fair nor dark, but an uncompromising brown.

So what was to be done? Enterprisingly — for Gareth was a prize worth risking everything for — Becky spent more than she could afford on women's magazines and scanned the 'Problem Pages'.

Blow! She had missed going out at day-break on May Day to bathe her face in the morning dew. That would have ensured her guaranteed beauty for the whole of the coming year, but she would have to rely on something else now. She began splashing her face with cold water to tone the skin, and rinsing her hair with the juice of a lemon to give it sheen and shine. Unfortunately, there seemed to be no difference to speak of to her appearance.

But she had managed to make contact with Gareth, who had joined the Youth Club and the Tennis Club, and had slotted into life in her quiet provincial village as though he had always belonged there. He had spoken to her six times already, and on one never-to-be-forgotten occasion had told her how much he admired her reading of *The Garden of Proserpine* when the Youth Club held a Literary Evening. But much to her chagrin, Marlene had managed a whole two hours alone with the softly spoken Celt, being given instruction on the constellations from the top of Beacher Hill.

"But he never — well — tried anything. He just talked about the stars until I was so bored I could have screamed," Marlene told a breathless audience of girls disappointedly later. Becky drew in her breath. How much more magical Aldebaran and Cassiopiae, the Pleiades and the passionate flame of the Evening Star would seem if she had heard her prince speak of them. (By now, she had discovered from her reading that everyone in the land of the Cymru could claim descent from the early Welsh princes! She had suspected he was royal from the start and this confirmed her suspicion.)

When mention was made of the Carnival her heart flared with hope. He hardly noticed her, in spite of the latest pale lipstick that gave her interestingly luminous eyes and a white mouth. She had even tried a rinse on her hair that was supposed to produce 'flattering auburn highlights' but even though the result was more orange than auburn, he did not seem to notice that she looked different. If she could get his attention it would be at the Carnival, especially if she could somehow contrive to be one of the Carnival Queens — .

It was a breathless and fairy-tale hope that she did not really believe in herself, but amazingly enough, the dream came true. It was all part of the magic of that summer. Councillor Dwight, a stout, balding man who seemed too old to Becky to be paying compliments, announced at the Carnival Planning

Party that Rebecca Golightly had been unanimously elected as the Rose Queen.

" — and we anticipate she will make just as beautiful a Rose Queen as her mother, who was Rose Queen for the Aldergate Carnival in — well, there, I won't embarrass her by mentioning the date," he declared jovially, adding: "It seems like yesterday, that's all I can say."

Becky looked at the stout figure with narrowed eyes. Somehow she knew intuitively.

"That man was in love with Mother. He loved her then — and he still does."

It was a sobering and dismaying thought, arousing all kinds of disturbing possibilities. But she pushed them to one side in the glory of the moment. Rose Queen! She would be the most glamorous Rose Queen there had ever been. Gareth would not be able to take his eyes from her.

Preparations for the Carnival sent her spirits soaring. Her dress had a low neck, for one thing, and she was also to be allowed to wear 'discreet make-up'. She took the bus to the nearest town and spent extravagantly at Woolworths. The

141

night before the Carnival, she was so excited she felt ill. Watching the sun set outside her window, she seemed to be cartwheeling head over heels and to be hearing voices that weren't there. One had to suffer to earn one's heart's desire.

She had chicken pox and even though the fever left her, she had to stay in quarantine with her spots. Tears spilled down onto her hands, clasped on the window ledge as she listened to the music blaring from the Carnival ground. She was not to worry, they said, Marlene looked lovely as Rose Queen in her place, and even Gareth and his parents, who had condescended to take the hoop-la stall, had commented on how attractive her blonde locks looked crowned with pink roses.

"It — it comes out of a bottle," Becky choked into her fist. She would never have dreamed of giving her friend away, of course, but sometimes it was so difficult to be honourable. She wanted to call down curses from the black clouds and sulphuric lightning to reduce the village to a charred waste. Marlene and the pink roses most of all.

So there was only one thing for it. She made her preparations with care, and planned for the evening of the day the quarantine ended. She told her mother she was going to attend the Tennis Club Dance, but Becky had more serious matters on her mind. She was going to throw herself over the edge of the Quarry.

It would be a sacrifice on the altar of love; a 'sop to fortune'. But he was worth it all. His very presence in her life had showed her that there were no limits to dreams and hopes and aspirations, no limits to all that was finest and most noble in the mind and heart of man. She would go willingly.

She put on an old white dress — white for her purity and her virginity. It clung plainly to her body, stirring a little in the gathering night breeze. Her arms were bare, and at the last moment, she added the Snake Bracelet that had been her mother's. She felt she was sharing in her mother's terrible grief by wearing something her father had given his love when he was alive.

The illness had left her a little thinner,

a little more pale. The orange highlights had gone from her hair, and it fell loose, thick and brown. She left the lip-stick on her dressing-table.

She called "Bye" to her mother, trying to sound normal, but very conscious that nothing about this night could be normal. The sun was setting in a blaze of fire and on the other side of the sky the Evening Star hung, mystic and magical. She walked in the direction of the Tennis Club, dust scuffing with the light movements of her thin sandals and settling on her bare feet. The air was balmy, heavy with perfume and promise. Becky's heart broke silently within her. It was enough.

It was quite a long walk to the edge of the Quarry, and she was alone in the amethyst twilight. She plucked dog roses from the hedge and set them in her hair. It was almost over.

And then, at the gate, she stopped. There was a figure barring her way. Tall, dark, with the legions of ghostly warriors at his back.

"Are you Morgan le Fay risen again to enchant my soul and bewitch me so that I shall never be free?"

Becky said nothing.

"I have missed you. Your mother thought you might come here, so I came first. Would you like to walk?"

"Yes please," she whispered, impatiently brushing away a few looming ravens of doubt and suspicion and mistrust.

He smiled down at her, touching her hair.

"Look, the stars will be out soon. Shall we go to look at them from the Hill?"

"Aldebaran, Cassiopiae, the Pleiades, the Great Bear," her mind repeated, dazed with wonder. The words sounded remarkably like a spell for obtaining your heart's desire.

Summing up Capricorn
(Dec 22 – Jan 20)

Lucky colours: Indigo, green, brown.

Gems: Black diamond, jet, rock crystal, obsidian, onyx.

Tarot card: The Devil.

Body parts controlled by Capricorn: skin, knees, bones.

Plants: Birch, Indian hemp.
Element: Earth.
Animal: Goat, ass, snow goose.
Perfume: Musk.
Ruler: Saturn.
Roman god: Bacchus.
Greek god: Pan.
Egyptian god: Khem.
Characteristics: Goal-orientated, ambition, toughness, endurance, sense of duty, irrational interests, hard work, seriousness, selfishness, objectivity, industriousness, materialism, loyalty, inflexibility, tenacity, loneliness.

The Nature spirits of Earth and Rock teach you to receive and transmit. Potentially powerful yet the fluidity of the feminine nature of this sign softens. Clear proper conduct brings high esteem from others. Ceremonies and privileges are appreciated. Little time for fun until later years.

Toughness and endurance can be spoiled by pride and possessions. Often your deep emotions are not acknowledged by others. It is better to be direct and open but there is innate shyness to overcome.

Aquarius
(Jan 21 – Feb 19)

SUN in Aquarius. Air, Fixed, Positive.

You are very concerned with bringing to the attention of the many, the ideas, or knowledge, of the few. You see ideas as being the natural property of the world at large and, in the propagation and spreading of them, you will effectively become the servant of whatever cause you champion.

In other words, you will subordinate your individuality to a wider group. The reason for this is your tendency to view society itself as a collective which must accommodate the individual, not as a collective that might create a series of individuals. Nevertheless, the pursuance of universal knowledge takes society into ever more virgin territory, and you are much committed to minimising the distance between man and his future.

You tend to be drawn into issues

of social concern; to institutionalise individuals in order to catagorise them. You are intellectual and detached, actively involved in the external world and endlessly socialising.

You can express extreme patterns of industriousness and 'laid backness'. The former brings constant physical activity resulting in a permanent 'busyness', as if one were 'housekeeping' one's way through life. The latter can incur a charge of apathy and slothfulness, all activity being seen as varying degrees of strenuous effort.

Your physical appeal can also be one of two extremes though often the more aesthetic type prevails. You are generally regarded as eccentric in the extreme — or at the very least, odd or different.

In spite of the brilliance and originality of your thinking, pronounced intellectual capacity is not necessarily your feature, though the willingness to hold to your ideas and stand your ground whatever the opposition, can acquire for you the accolade of possessing an unchallengeable moral power.

You have an unconventional humanitarian

approach to life and are rarely shocked by the foibles of others. You are likely to have many friends but to steer clear of deeply intimate romantic encounters, as the one thing you dread above all is revealing your feelings to others.

★ ★ ★

The introduction to TEA FOR TWO shows the multi-level approach of the Aquarian mind. Issues of emotion, heart, spirit-soul, body-blood and even time itself — lifespans — are raised. Even the issue of identity, involvement and detachment are hinted at through the use of the concept of proxy.

Observation, existence, relationship and circumstance blend to reveal patterns shown by planetary influences.

Environmental issues are discussed, bringing into focus motivational matters, ideals and political realities. The mis-understood outsider gives us new insights and viewpoints into the ways of the world, rewriting the rulebook of behaviourism.

Delegation to servants and the giving

of service lend flavour to this telling
tale.

Tea For Two

Tea for two, and some cakes.
You take even the words out of my
mouth, don't you? Anything else you
want? My heart — or what's left of it?
My soul — if I have a soul? Why not
help yourself to my blood, guzzling in a
glitter of vampirish teeth, sinking them
into my neck? Am I going to have the
remaining years of life taken from me
now, to be lived by proxy through you?

I look round. It's quite a pleasant
place, this, isn't it? Oh, but I don't
suppose you've noticed. You don't live
in the world, do you? You simply exist,
and everything has to revolve around you
— suns, moons, stars, the lot. What gave
you that terrible selfishness, I wonder, to
take it for granted you're the centre of
the universe?

I'd like to stand up here in this
olde-worlde English tea-shoppe and tell
everybody what you really are, what

150

you've done to me. How shocked they'd be. That horsed-faced woman over there in the corner, embroiled in pamphlets about Protecting the Environment. That couple with purple hair by the window holding hands, gazing into each other's eyes. I don't think they'd be bothered, on second thoughts. They're completely wrapped up in each other. In love. Hah! Love!

Are you sure the cream's fresh?

Of course she's sure, you suspicious old hag. What's the poem, something about two men looking out through prison bars — 'one saw mud, the other saw stars'. I know just what the author meant.

If they look at us, what do they see? A dear white-haired couple sitting companionably, not talking because, over the years, we've learned to communicate without words. Hah! You're wrong! All wrong! We don't talk because we've got nothing to say to each other. I've had nothing to say to her for an eternity now. I'd bite off my tongue rather than speak to her.

Look at her! Sitting there like a fat

151

leech, blinking behind those terrible spectacles. There's something almost disarming about her utter repulsiveness, isn't there? Maybe one could learn to regard her as a sort of gargoyle, grow fond of her ugliness. Fat — complacent, unfeeling — a death's head at the feast — you could get accustomed to that in a way, couldn't you? You could maybe, but not me. I look at that thick pasty face and I see tears, I see the last time she ever had any feelings, the time she cried. Splotches of red mottling her skin, eyes bloodshot and slimy, mouth sagging open.

I love you, you snivelled. I love you James, don't be so cold. I can't bear it. You've never looked more hideous than you did that day, old woman.

She sits there, staring at nothing, picking up the cup in her slug-like fingers, slurping the tea with her slug-like mouth. Did anyone ever kiss that mouth? What a thought! It makes me want to retch.

And, stealing like an elusive fragrance from the past, I'm saved, kissing the lips of my Lucy again — warm, tremulous, sweet as water in the desert to a dying man. She was all fair hair and pink skirts and flowers, my Lucy. A slip of a girl with eyes you wanted to drown in and skin like summer rain. And when she smiled — .

Pass the sugar please.

Here it is, you old witch. You need it, bowls and bowls full of sugar to sweeten all that sourness out of you. Lot's wife turned into salt, didn't she? Hah! Lot was lucky.

So now I'm getting blasphemous. What would your esteemed father have said to that, I wonder? Simpering other-world clergyman with his snowy hair and vague useless smile. I wish he were here now so that I could shock him, shout at him. Damn her! Damn her! That's right, sir. That's exactly what I said, sir. Damn and blast your bloody daughter to hell, sir!

More tea, James?

What's what my Lucy used to say. More tea, James? Her frail little voice like a bell. When she laughed, it was as though a flock of birds, white birds were soaring through the sky. When she was sad, it was like listening to solemn music.

Hideous old hypocrite. What right have you to use her words? They come out of your mouth filthy because you've said them, smirched by your flabby chins and your fat flesh, freckled and clammy as a toad.

She sits there, an obscene Buddah, sprawling her legs disgustingly to make room for her belly. My Lucy was like a reed, so slim, so dainty. I could almost span her waist with my hands. Her breasts were as soft as young birds, and her legs were like new saplings. She had the face of an angel. That girl over there has something of her look. Perhaps her daughter would have looked like that now — or her grand-daughter — if she'd had a daughter — .

Thank God you never bred, old woman. You'd have produced monsters if you hadn't been barren as a rock. Stones and pebbles for your sons, tears for your daughters — those same tears that streaked your face like the tracks left by a snail.

But we have each other, James, you whimpered. Hah! I don't have you, don't want you, wouldn't take you on a silver

154

platter. How could any man ever want you? And you'll never have me. I belong to my Lucy, body and soul, I always will. We gave ourselves to each other sealed the pact with a ring of grass, plaited, warmed with the sun of youth. Oh, sacred meeting of soft lips, steadiness of love in her eyes and in mine. I can feel that moment now. When she lived, breathed, smiled — my Lucy, joy of my heart, light of my life — my Lucy, gone from me for ever leaving only this aching void, this impotent shaking of my fist at the gods — .

Look at you, a crumb in the corner of your mouth and sweating like a pig. How can you bear to live with yourself when you reek like that, old woman?

Lucy was fragile as a memory, sweet with the fragrance of gardenia. I'd send them to her when I was away. Boxes and boxes of white gardenias with their big satin bows, their moss and fern, cool as a woody glade, fugitive as hot-houses in summer. Gardenias in crystal vases bring her back even now, summon up her dear lost wraith — . But for you, old hag, I'd pluck the fiercest of stinging nettles,

155

deadly nightshade, poisonous fungi.

Coleridge's wasn't the only ancient mariner to have an albatross settle round his neck. Or a mill-stone. But I'm old — old — and it's weary to hate like this. Do you age, old wretch? Weren't you always old, loathsome and mottled? Didn't you crawl from some unspeakable den exactly as you are? You could never have been young, never have laughed, worn pink dresses, smelled of gardenia? Could you? Could you?

It's like watching some deformed thing trying to move when she gets up. But don't dare to come near me. Don't dare to put those flabby hands on me. I'm not so decrepit that I'll accept your touch, crawling on my skin.

She knows. She waits. And suddenly, blindingly, I see the sadness in the eyes behind those awful spectacles.

I'll pay the waitress while you get your coat on, James.

Oh, Lucy, Lucy! Where did we go wrong? Where did we lose each other? Oh, my Lucy, forgive me — forgive me — !

Summing up Aquarius
(Jan 21 – Feb 19)

Element: Air.
Lucky gem: Quartz crystal.
Colour: Blue.
Lucky number: 4.
Flower: Primrose.
Planet: Uranus.
Metal: Lead.
Tarot card: The Star.
Animals: Peacock, eagle.
Aquarius rules: Back, circulation, breathing.
Key words: 'I know'.
Characteristics: Original, metaphysical, humane, independent, inventive.
Negative: Eccentric, rebellious, detached.
This is the sign of the genius, the 'mad professor', the inventor of magical toys. There is much in Aquarius that is fresh and new, yet it is a fixed sign, which means that the ideas signified by its element Air are inclined to remain fixed. Consequently, Aquarians can be surprisingly reluctant to change their views, and can even veer towards

157

conservatism in many aspects of their lives.

They love mysteries and have tremendously inquiring minds. Letting them catch a glimpse of 'a secret' is a sure way to gain their undivided attention.

They are of two sorts — the smooth and the sloppy. 'Smooth' Aquarians project an impression of unusual but elegant taste. 'Sloppy' Aquarians are surrounded by clutter and unidentifiable, half-completed objects they have invented or might find a use for.

Aquarians have an intense awareness of self, and their lives reflect a journey towards wisdom. This is the sign marking the unifying of the waters of life and knowledge. Aquarius is conscious that it carries gifts for the world.

Pisces
(Feb 20 – March 20)

SUN in Pisces. Your biggest problem lies in achieving a sense of reality. You constantly receive impressions of life and may unconsciously absorb the personalities of others. You can be lazy and easy going to near martyrdom, allowing others to walk all over you, and there may be a tendency to overindulge in drink and other forms of escapism.

You have tremendous artistic and poetic abilities and strong sympathy with those who are suffering, but you must be careful that self pity does not lead to diffusion of purpose and breaks in concentration.

You are lucky in political affairs. World changes are disruptive but work to your advantage eventually.

Sun in Pisces is Water, Mutable, Negative. Yours being the last sign of the zodiac, it is inevitable that many features from preceding Sun Signs should have their residue in Pisces. This gene link can be burdensome and produce chaos, or it can give you a broad church of intuitive understanding and an intellectual capacity of unusual dimension.

Such a width, when coupled with the receptive qualities of your element, Water, often make it possible for you to be very open to extra-dimension activity — styled spiritualism perhaps making you an unusually effective medium.

But Water can also have its negative expression: a wild emotionalism, producing an inability to discriminate the value of things, can give you a tendency sometimes to respond to illusory causes with an unwarranted degree of enthusiasm.

★ ★ ★

My choice of story for this sign, THE BRIDGE, is a successfully creepy tale which embodies both the extra-sensitivity that can enable those born under Pisces to exist in many worlds, and in this case, the sinister effect their ability to absorb the personalities of others might have on their own destiny.

Even the fact that one of the central features is a bridge across a wild and chaotic stretch of water is indicative of the mutability and mysterious nature of this sign. We are not sure, even when the tale is told, how much was real and how much might have been imagination. Pisces is not always as doom-laden as this and if the outcome had been happy instead of tragic, it would have gone to the opposite extreme and enabled the heroine, on the same illusory evidence, to have settled into delirious bliss. Often with Pisces, it is a case of their creating their destinies themselves, and a little positive thinking can go a long way. For those who prefer to star in tragic drama, however, the stage waits and the Greek chorus, heads veiled, are always ready to welcome the martyr.

The Bridge

'A rather lovely spot in Wales,' was how Roddy'd described it, but as she stood on the bridge staring out over the ravine where the stream — or river, or whatever it was — tumbled picturesquely over black rocks, many feet below, and the hills opened out on either side, thickly wooded, with a sort of amethyst haze beyond that hinted at higher and wilder mountains misted by distance and the heat, Jane's first thought was:

"What a place for a murder!"

It gave her a creepy chill down her spine, in spite of the sunlight that fell in dappled shapes through the boughs overhead onto the moss-encrusted stonework of the bridge. An old bridge, just like the Lodge; she wondered what the Hall itself had been like. Long gone, Roddy had told her, though some of the rare shrubs that had made up the gardens remained, and he'd already pointed out the rhododendron bushes along the side of the ravine from the Lodge window. She couldn't wait to go out and explore, so she'd left him cursing the phone call that had interrupted their first morning, putting notes and papers together to get them in the post.

"I suppose it's still Pony Express here," Jane said demurely, and he scowled.

162

"I'll have to take the car to the Post Office. D'you want to come?"

"No, I'm going to brave the ghosts of Owen Glendower and whoever else haunts the ravine," she said, thinking as she'd thought last night when they arrived in the dark, that after London, you could simply drink the air here, it was like wine. Maybe you could get drunk on it, Welsh Wales was potent stuff.

She hadn't been too keen on the idea of coming to an isolated valley when Roddy had first mentioned it. Somewhere like Majorca or Malta, where her brothers took their families, had been what she'd have liked, but Roddy wouldn't hear of such a thing. He put on what she was beginning to think of as his 'aristocratic' expression of hauteur, and stated disagreeably:

"I dislike mingling with the common herds, my love. The cottage is ideally situated, extremely peaceful in beautiful surroundings; it used to be the Lodge of one of the area's most noted stately homes."

So of course, she'd agreed that it would

be the best possible place for them to celebrate the legality of their union after two years of unwed romance. She very rarely did object when Roddy held forth, it had got to be a habit; after all, he'd always been her boss, and she'd been his acquiescent secretary.

"Yes, Mr Lawford."

"No, Mr Lawford."

Jane ran her hand absently along the top of the stonework of the bridge, allowing herself to admit in the rustling serenity of this beautiful morning that in her secret heart, she was deeply thankful — and more than thankful, *relieved* — that Roddy had taken the trouble to arrange this holiday (a sort of delayed honeymoon) at all. Dalliance with his young secretary — the opportunity to display his affluence and power and prestige to a dazzled girl had suited Roddy down to the ground, and he'd benevolently showered her with roses and perfume, swept her off her feet with an unsuspected sensuousness and passion that didn't seem to fit his impregnable business image at all. But after she made what he coldly referred to as 'her mistake',

164

and due to carelessness (well, that was what he'd said, though she suspected he was certain she'd done it deliberately) she thought she'd become pregnant, and he'd arranged a hasty wedding, something of the benevolence disappeared completely, and she discovered to her dismay that she was married to a rather frightening stranger.

When they found out there wasn't going to be a baby at all, she even enquired hesitantly whether he regretted the marriage, whether he'd like a divorce, since it was so easy now to get them.

He'd stared at her with an enigmatic expression before he asked in low, measured tones:

"You want to leave me?"

Jane turned back to her mirror, fiddled with the brushes on her elaborate dressing-table.

"I rather imagined it was the other way about, that you'd have been glad to get rid of *me*." She tried for a light, sophisticated touch. "Don't worry, I'll go quietly, if that's what you think would be best."

Irony was lost on Roddy, though.

She'd found since their marriage that the pedantic way he had of speaking wasn't just a dry and witty take-off of men with less of a sense of humour — which she'd always thought, blinded, she supposed by the excitement of their affair — but exactly what it appeared to be. Really, he wasn't half as interesting a person as he'd seemed when it was just a boss-and-secretary thing. And with the show of amiability gone, the only thing that seemed to be left was the blank, cold facade he showed his business competitors. Jane had no idea what lay behind it, and she wasn't sure she wanted to find out. Ruthlessness, she supposed, anger at the way he thought she'd tricked him into making her his wife. Even the way he stared at her now, with a sort of hungry calculation in his eyes, gave her an uneasy feeling.

"You'll go nowhere, my love," he said softly, after he'd considered her last remark. "My family, as you know, is a very old and highly esteemed one. My mother would never condone a divorce for a moment. When a Lawford marries, it's for life."

But there was something in his voice — a hint of doubt, perhaps? — that lodged in Jane's mind and wouldn't be shifted. For life, he'd declared implacably, yet the emotion behind those words — something she couldn't identify — continued to bother Jane. She couldn't have said exactly in what way it bothered her, but she had been sure it was a glimpse she'd had of some very deeply hidden feeling Roddy was concealing, maybe the anger she was afraid he might let loose in some terrifying way one day. She drew more and more aloof, defensive, became wary, but to her dismay, he seemed to become compensatingly more possessive — it gave her the impression she was being trapped.

But now, as she gazed with troubled and unseeing eyes across the ravine, where the water leaped and sparkled silver in the sunlight, she felt something of an easing of the bonds. It was so beautifully free here. Perhaps the marriage hadn't been such a mistake after all. Perhaps Roddy had forgiven her, perhaps now that he'd managed to make the time to leave the business in

Tim's hands for a couple of weeks, and could afford to relax a bit, he'd get back some of the benevolence of the years of romance, and stop giving her the feeling of being hounded by a ferocious depth of emotion held in check.

She absently switched her gaze lower to the shadow of the bridge as it fell across the water, and for a minute or two, though her eyes reported to her brain what she was seeing, her mind wouldn't take it in. It was something beyond her comprehension on this lovely summer morning, with birds singing in the trees all round. To see, far below, the body of a woman lying in the shallows.

The face was turned down, the fast-flowing stream rippling on either side of it, pulling at the darkened hair and making it move slightly. One hand was thrown out, the other hidden beneath her. She was wearing something vaguely light-coloured, but her legs were visible, wavering beneath the surface, her feet bare. Jane stood, staring, before the wave of sickness hit her, knowing with absolute certainty that the woman was dead. Only the water moved, gurgling past, tugging at the hair, giving an illusion of life.

She had managed to reach the Lodge, fifty yards further up the road past the bridge, and had actually picked up the hand-set of the phone to call the police, when Roddy came into the room, and, seeing the whiteness of her face, the shock in her eyes, demanded suspiciously:

"What's the matter? What are you doing?"

Jane said shakily:

"There's a body in the water — under the bridge. I'm calling the — ."

With a muttered exclamation, he strode across and snatched the hand-set from her, replaced it with a clatter.

"Now, pull yourself together. You're hysterical."

Jane sat shivering.

"What's all this about a body?" he demanded.

"In the water. Under the bridge." Her teeth were chattering. She felt very cold.

"Show me," he said after a moment, and she rose on quivering legs and took a few deep breaths before she walked from the room and led the way into the flagged hall and out through the front door.

Roddy couldn't have been kinder when they got back, and she was tempted to forget those awful moments when he had snatched the phone from her, with no thought apparently for her weak state and the horror of what she had just seen. Because, as he patiently explained while she sipped the brandy he brought, it had obviously all been her imagination. Since there was certainly no body in the water, what else could it have been?

Jane pulled the blanket he'd draped round her shoulders closer to her.

"It wasn't imagination," she said stubbornly. "I know what I saw, and I still think we should call the police. Just in case. She — it might have been moved — ."

"My dear girl." Roddy was at his most paternal, playing up what he usually liked to ignore, the difference in their ages. "Who could have moved it? If it was there, even? It takes quite a time to climb down into the ravine, and you didn't see anyone else, did you?"

She hated to admit it, but she had to be honest, and shook her head reluctantly.

"There was nobody — only her, lying there."

He laid a heavy hand on her shoulder, and she felt a sudden urge to shrug it off.

"These last few months have been a terrible strain for you, my love," he said. "I'm hoping you'll recover yourself now we're here. A few weeks of solitude — ."

"A few weeks?" Jane cried. "You've got to be joking. I'm not staying here another night. I — it was an awful experience, and I — I want to go home."

To her shame, her voice wobbled dangerously, but Roddy only lifted his hand from her shoulder to stroke her fair hair, loosened untidily round her face.

"Would you like me to call a doctor?" he asked, and she bit back the retort that sprang to her lips, gritting her teeth before she managed to say, with admirable calm:

"Roddy, please stop treating me like a child. I've had a shock, and I'm a little — well, shaken up. How can I stay here, right next to the bridge, where every time I go for a walk, I'll be expecting to see — her — in the water again?"

"But you looked just now, with me, and there was nothing there," he pointed out. "There's no need to feel you're going to see anything again, why should you?"

Jane looked at him suddenly, straight in the eye.

"Tell me the truth. Has anyone ever died like that in the stream? Is it a ghost? Is the place haunted, is that why you're being so intolerably patient and understanding?"

There was a silence, then his eyes slid away.

"Not — so far as I know," he said, but Jane didn't believe him. She sighed, relieved. If it was a ghost, if that was all, if it was simply the replaying of an old, past tragedy, then there was no need to worry.

"Why didn't you tell me?" she asked, and he countered innocently:

"Tell you what, my love?"

"Oh, forget it," Jane said shortly. "You'd better get on with whatever you were doing — going to the Post Office with those papers for Tim."

By the next morning, she felt a great

deal better, and was able to view the whole thing in a more rational perspective. She'd had a good night, surprisingly, since she expected to be haunted by visions of the woman lying in the water, but with the dawn of a new day, fresh and warm again, her spirits rose. One could accept a ghost, couldn't one, even though Roddy obviously didn't want to discuss the matter. In fact, something — probably what had happened to her, what she'd seen — seemed to be bothering him more than it was bothering her. He hardly spoke during breakfast, and when she suggested a walk, he demurred and said he'd read the papers he'd brought with him.

"You go, my love."

"Well, all right," Jane agreed, wishing she could drive, then at least she'd be able to get out of this valley to civilization for an hour or two, instead of pottering round on her own. She wouldn't go past the bridge, not today — though when she set out, that was where her feet led her, and, her heart in her mouth, she peered with fascinated horror over the parapet expecting to see the woman there again, but the stream was empty. After that, Jane felt her confidence surging back. It had just been an isolated incident, it wouldn't happen again. In a way, she even began to feel rather smug about it, though her sense of unease remained — there had been a coldness, something inexplicably ghastly about recalling the moment she'd actually seen the ghost. But it didn't happen to everyone, did it? Not a real haunting. With all the chills and terrors you expected.

As she walked on along the empty road — very few cars ever came this way, it was strangely silent after London, and Jane found it disturbing to be so alone, though the scenery was beautiful, of course — she started to wonder whether Roddy had ever seen the ghost. He must have, she thought, or else he would have scoffed at her suggestion that the place was haunted. He probably knew what had happened, who the woman had been. She felt curious herself, but was reluctant to ask him about it. There had been a look in his eyes as they sat at breakfast that had revived all the doubts that had been building up since their marriage, a sort of measuring, speculative look. A very odd look, when she came to think about it. As though Roddy had come to a momentous decision, as though he'd been mulling something over in his mind and it had reached fruition, and he had some plan, he intended to take action. She shivered suddenly, though the sun was hot. She was sure the action was directed against herself. Last night, for instance, when she'd expected him to want to make love to her as a sort of gesture to celebrate their escape from the grind of work and London, he'd been very withdrawn, hadn't seemed interested. And yet he'd said himself that the holiday was supposed to help them recover their closeness, not to drive them further apart. But just at this moment, surrounded by the strangeness of wild hills, aware of her solitude, she did feel very much alone.

It wasn't a pleasant feeling, and her thoughts slowed her steps, brought her to a halt. There was a large stone not far away, at the side of the road, thickly grown about with grass and wild flowers that Jane didn't know the names of. She made dash for it and sat down, trying to tell herself that she was enjoying this opportunity to breathe in the sweetly scented country air (like wine?) and watch a white butterfly dance erratically past, on across the ravine. Her eyes followed it, to her left where the road curved to the bridge, and she gave a little choked cry, and stiffened. She was a long way off — she'd walked some distance up the road — but she could see the stream emerge from the shadows, and there was — wasn't there? — a huddled figure down in the depths of the water, the gleam of the woman's pale garment.

Jane got shakily to her feet, a hand at her mouth, her heart beating fast. There *was* somebody there, lying still and silent, and the same horror and nausea that had swept over her yesterday hit her once again. The clear sky seemed to darken, a sense of menace gripped her. What *was* this? What was happening? Was she going crazy?

She forced herself to sit back on the stone and wait until her panic ebbed and her ragged breathing slowed. Deliberately, she did not look in the direction of the bridge again. But as she summoned her courage to make the return journey along the road, to actually cross that awful bridge in order to reach the haven of the Lodge once more, she made up her mind that whatever Roddy said, she'd insist on returning to London immediately. And if he didn't want to, if he wanted to stay here in this gruesome place, he could drive her to the nearest station to catch a train. If she had to keep putting up with shocks like this, her nerves would crack. She had enough to think about trying to sort out the problems of her marriage, heaven knew, without being terrified out of her wits by being continually haunted.

Once having made her decision, she felt better and got up, shaking out the folds of her cotton skirt. She began to stride back the way she had come, forcing herself not to look — not even to glance — into the shadows below the bridge. When she reached the corner and had to cross the bridge itself, she turned the curve, and in a sudden panic, ran all the way across and up to the Lodge, even though the unaccustomed effort brought a stitch to her side and left her shaking and panting. But she was safely in the Lodge garden, and she stopped beside the gnarled old tree that over-hung the porch and clutched at the trunk for support, holding on and shutting her eyes, until the faintness passed.

But when she opened her eyes, her relief was shattered. She caught a glimpse of Roddy purposefully striding towards the house from the other side of the garden — and he was carrying, of all things, a spade fresh with new earth. Roddy, who never in his life ever soiled his hands with manual work. Without conscious thought, Jane shrank behind the tree, really frightened, as a wild realisation bloomed in her brain, and screamed itself across her whole consciousness.

"He's been digging — . He's been digging my grave!"

And it all fell into place. The strange look in his eyes at breakfast, his preoccupation with some dark matter that she could not share, the sense of being wounded, pursued, threatened.

Jane's mind threw the picture of the woman in the water up at her, and she knew suddenly that Roddy had good reason for wanting to keep the police away from the Lodge. He'd killed that woman! Jane bit her lip so that it bled. She was married to a murderer, and he'd brought her here to this awful desolate empty valley to get rid of her!

She couldn't move, couldn't think. She clung to the tree for what seemed hours, trying to catch her breath, steady herself so that she could run — run anywhere — get away — away from him — . Steady, Jane, she managed to tell herself, thinking frantically of the need for money, she'd want her bag first, and then — .

Roddy's voice spoke from the other side of her. Oh, God, he'd gone round the house, he must have seen her hiding behind the tree — !

"Did you enjoy your walk, my love?"

Jane was afraid she might faint as she turned, still clinging to the trunk, and faced him.

"I'm a bit — tired. I ran part of the way."

At least the words came out, though she was uncomfortably aware that the scream behind them had only been repressed with an extreme effort, but he didn't seem to notice anything wrong.

"You ran?"

His smile, that didn't reach his eyes.

"Yes, I — just felt like running. Exercise, you know."

Don't let him guess, don't let him suspect!

"I've been busy too," he said. "Something unusual for me. I've been digging the garden."

"Oh?"

How predatory his teeth were! How cold his eyes! How thin his lips! She shook as he came forward and grasped her arm, led her through the porch into the house while she tried desperately not to shrink away from his touch.

"Lunch is all ready," he said, guiding her into the sitting-room with its mullioned windows set in thick stone walls. Jane gulped the coolness of the shady room, hoping she wouldn't be sick at the sight of the food. "There, I'm getting domesticated, aren't I, my love? I thought we'd have salad."

Poison? Jane wondered frantically. She wouldn't risk even a mouthful.

"I'm — I'm not really very hungry," she managed, and he frowned.

"You don't look well. You're a little pale. Would you like a drink?"

Her bag, she thought, where was her bag with her money, her credit cards? Then she remembered it was on the oak chest in the hall. She could do it, she could get away, and once free of the house, she'd plunge into the trees somewhere and be able to dodge him. Got to keep calm, though, act the part right or you're done for, Jane.

She sank down shakily — more shakily than she really was, since her whole being was keyed up to make a mad as soon as he went out of the room — and tasted the blood from her lip as she mouthed:

"Oh, yes, a drink. Thank you — ."

"I'll get it," he said, but didn't move for a moment. He stood looking down at her with a sort of regretful expression. She felt herself wanting to scream, to

181

laugh, she could hardly contain her wild panic. Was he feeling sorry he'd got to kill her? Sorry for her, or for himself? Her skin crawled, she could feel the chair quivering beneath her.

"I've been thinking things out," he said, and then turned abruptly, to her shuddering relief, and went into the kitchen. She didn't wait but leaped to her feet, rushed through the hall, snatched up her bag and darted like a hunted animal through the garden, down the road and across the bridge.

The driver of the red sports car, unfamiliar with the road, was taking the corner too fast, he was already trying to reduce speed, and when he saw the woman in the white dress running apparently straight into his path he tried to swerve to avoid her. But all the same, he hit her, and even as the car skidded to a halt he knew it was too late. She'd been thrown against the barbed wire fence that followed the stonework of the bridge across the grassy incline, tumbled awkwardly to fall beyond it, then unable to stop herself, had begin to roll down. And after a few yards, the grass gave way to the sheer edge of the ravine.

The driver's hoarse yell of warning, the grinding of brakes, the long-drawn "Aaaahhhh!" as she fell roused the birds, and they flew up from the trees, chattering and screeching. Then, since there was no further sound, they began to settle again.

Roddy, white-faced, stood with the driver on the parapet, both paralysed into immobility as they stared into the depths. Her bag and mule sandals were scattered on the grassy bank. She was oblivious, far below.

The face was turned down, the fast-flowing stream rippling on either side of it, pulling at the darkened hair and making it move slightly. One hand was thrown out, the other hidden beneath her. She was wearing something vaguely light-coloured, but her legs were visible, wavering beneath the surface, her feet bare. Only the water moved, gurgling past, tugging at the hair, giving an illusion of life.

Summing up Pisces
(Feb 20 – March 20)

Element: Water.
Planet: Neptune.
Colour: Green.
Lucky number: 7.
Plant: Bergamot.
Perfume: Ambergris.
Gems: Pearl, amethyst, aquamarine.
Metal: Tin.
Animals: Fish, dolphin.
Tarot card: The Moon.
Pisces rules: The feet and toes.
Key words: 'I believe'.
Characteristics: Compassionate, sensitive, creative, mystical.
Negative: Indecisive, confused, vague.

As this is a Mutable sign it is changeable, and the Piscean can change almost from moment to moment. He is inclined to live in his own private world of sensitivity, compassion and love, and will need to work hard to link this with reality and to control his tendency to wallow in emotional trauma and excess, whether his own or that of others.

Pisceans are usually extremely artistic

and make good actors as they feel at home in a world of fantasy. They love children and may shine in caring or counselling work.

They live with constant emotional undercurrents as they drift through the wide seas of thought and mystery, driven by the wind of their brimming compassion for others.

The Authors, By Each Other

Richard Lawler, Astrologer — Aquarius
by Dilys Gater

RICHARD is far more Aquarian than any human being has a right to be. When he walks out of any door, I have a distinct feeling that he may never come back, he might walk into another dimension, get kidnapped or accept a sudden interesting job in the Antarctic which necessitates leaving within ten minutes by private jet. I would not be surprised to hear that he has in fact actually done all of those things as well as a great many more. What I am saying is that he is as insubstantial as water, the 'aqua' of his sign, and as difficult to pin down as air.

He can go to sleep while you are talking to him or change the subject in mid-sentence, cutting you off, but amazingly, this rarely causes offence. He is interested in everything, and his interest never flags. It makes you see the world in a new light and appreciate the burning passions that illuminate Aquarius — all ideas that spring into his mind are concerned with the good of humanity, and often work to his own disadvantage. He is incredibly self-contained and yet is one of the least selfish people I have ever met.

He has an ability rare in most people — and especially rare in Aquarius — of not trying to interfere, organise or direct the lives and thoughts of others. He allows personal freedom to those around him and gives them room to grow. This kind of intuitive thoughtfulness can inspire great passion and devotion in others, or it can be regarded as weakness and a refusal to face responsibility. People often respond to Aquarius with either intense irritation or equally intense delight.

Richard is, like most Aquarians, probably a genius. He has already invented rockets, written poetry which would be stunningly brilliant if only he could take the time to polish it up, sampled the stage and film as actor, writer and director, touched the stars. But like all Aquarians, he is as diffuse as the wind. One foot is on the topmost rock of the last mountain he climbed, but the other is stepping onto a fleeting rainbow, while his eyes reach beyond the horizon and each hand goes out in a different direction for whatever they can catch, whether it be the alchemist's stone or a lost rose fallen from a dance corsage into the gutter of a dark city street after the last dance is over.

Richard can hear everything you say to him even if he is not listening. He can speak with the naïvety of a child — until you realise that everything he says has the sharpness and accuracy of a stiletto blade. He never plays games of one-upmanship — he has never heard of them. But then, he does not need to.

When you enter the world of an Aquarian, expect to have your realities turned upside down. Anything can happen. But two things I can guarantee — with Richard around, you will never grow old. And you will never be bored.

Dilys Gater, Author — Aries

by Richard Lawler

IN the stories told here, we have different character traits. Thus we see a consistency of thought, action, purpose, feelings and values. However people and their handwriting change from time to time, both in the short and long term.

Our authoress uses fantasy to bring her glowing characters for your entertainment. Every sign of the zodiac is a phantom in the sense that it is an absolute which is never attained.

Dilys has the Sun in Aries in the third Fire Sign along so her Aries sun has qualities of Sagittarius and in her early life she travelled around a lot offering agents and publishers her work.

Her Aquarian moon can make her detached and though an asset in the writing sphere because it allows her to stand outside situations, it has caused her some trouble in her friendships, affairs

189

and marriages. It is a cold erotic moon that can fulfil the desires of others but often sees emotions, beliefs and concepts in a way that is alien to those closest to her.

Mercury in Taurus allows Dilys to adapt to different environments and she is happiest in printers' offices and production premises, even when it is not her own work coming off the press!

Neptune in Libra gives a wide public appeal for her 65 published books — and hopefully the additional half dozen now in the pipeline.

Jupiter in Leo gives her a style in dress and she likes to rise to the occasion. She often wins prizes in raffles and quiz competitions as well as awards for her work. She was voted Woman of the Year 1994 in America recently, though she declined copies of the medal.

Mars in Cancer gives a streamlined home life. Currently she lives with two diamond doves who heckle her to remind her to return to Earth Base Planet 3 occasionally.

Saturn on the descendant shows that places like London and New York are structuring themselves for her work.

Venus in Aries gives a love of adventure and she has written books on pirates and land battles and even had fights with people who believe they have a monopoly of the facts! It brings her to the forefront, and her books on 'How to write' plays, novels and short stories, as well as the Writing Course material she has also written are in their own field on the best-seller lists. She has written many thousands of articles over the years, including a large percentage on 'How to Write'.

Uranus in Gemini explains her nom de plumes, which include: Olwen Edwards, Vivien Young, Clover Sinclair, Katrina Wright, Lys Holland and Dawn Rose.

The aspect here indicates she is on the brink of international acclaim in the television, media and radio worlds. Film producers please form an orderly queue — !

An Informal Personal View On How the Stars Work

by Richard Lawler

HOW do you become an astrologer? One can enroll in a reputable school or with an esteemed teacher. The mathematics is a bit daunting to the beginner and the interpretation depends on a process of analysis followed by synthesis and judgement.

Without a birth time 30% of the chart is lost, but the chart can be used to some extent. There are various sophisticated ways of guessing parts of a horoscope and working backwards to give a time of birth. Even some people who have precise birth times need to have their chart made to align better. This 'rectification' gives a better fit. In the same way some people can buy clothes off the peg, others need to get bespoke or tailor-made clothes.

Some people have a knack of calculation and I have written texts on mental arithmetic, studied vedic maths, and shaped courses on mental development. Nowadays the use of calculators and computers have been known to help people but I feel it is important to be able to get into chart calculations the hard way; because through this process the whole concept of time and weighting of partial factors takes place.

With interpretation, however good your astrology, you do need experience of life. It is possible to be an 'agony aunt' without any technical counselling skills, psychology training or astrological insight — however the better ones always have these skills.

Horo-scope means looking at the hour. Sometimes in life one does not have that long to avert a horror-scope scenario.

The anecdotes given below indicate some patterns that a skilled astrologer could detect. I am not going to go into all the links here but will let you discover them for yourselves. Even in apparently random emergencies there can be patterns in the dangers presented — even across two generations of family life.

My early life was very hard. I had a sister eight years older than me who was head girl at Putney High School; I had to compete with her for food — we were so poor after the war that we used to make houses out of playing cards and sugar ration stamps as we could not afford to buy sweets. In other ways. The competition was more insidious as she was able to gain points through her feminity and experience. She was very ambitious and desperate to leave home. I was always viewed as a threat to be eliminated and neutralised in any way possible. Often I had to deal with her many suitors after my mother had been tricked out on an errand or a mission of mercy. The description of myself given to her boyfriends was such as to occasion the most violent of reactions in these men. Often I could duck the blows and they would hit the wall but on occasion it was me that said hello to the wall and floor and then the emergency hospital and dental wards. On one occasion I was a bit ill to start with and my reaction speed was down and I did not quite sum up the situation quickly enough. Not that odd as I was delirious with a fever. A neighbour Winifred found me lying unconscious in a pool of blood missing a tooth.

Through this I had a near death experience that changed my viewpoint on life. While under dental gases I met with angels, fairies, pixies and elves. The gas turned out to be carbon dioxide and I had to have emergency heart massage when my heart stopped. These angelic friends have often come to me in times of need but only at their own discretion.

The astrologer is often sensitive but this is not strictly necessary as precedent and judgment can be used as in a legal process where tradition meets with convention to be assessed by a skilled arbitrator.

There are many factors in astrology and a chart is like a large ticking clock. If I had not been found after the assault I would not be here. If Mrs Vickers from the Parson's Green Maternity and Dental Clinic at Fulham had not recommended an emergency dental clinic in Leicester Square I could have bled to death before I got there. If my father had not been quickly able to borrow the money for a cab when an ambulance failed to arrive, I would not have lived.

But troubles rarely come singly and in real life fact can be stranger than fiction. The dental nurse was so distressed by my condition that she had linked up the wrong gas cylinders. The local ambulances were at a bad fire near where we lived and had been hemmed in by falling masonry.

Ironically one of my contract computing jobs was for the home office in Horseferry Road where I helped to design and program a 999 system of responses for the fire, ambulance and metropolitan police. This was so good that I was employed by International Air Radio to work on a radio version covering much more isolated areas in Winnipeg for the Canadian fire, ambulance and mounties.

While working on the 999 systems I had access to real times of calls and actual responses. At weekends I would use these times for astrological research as they were much more reliable than most birth times. Astrology is about any sort of event in time and this data was to help me bring comfort to more people.

Once there was a minor gas explosion in a house in Victoria, London. I knew there was a bad aspect at this time. A routine ambulance response was activated, the vehicle not being in any great hurry because there was no injury report. It crashed into a lamppost blocking the flow of traffic. Two police cars sent out to cover the ambulance were radioed to step on it to the RTA (road traffic accident) and turned into the same road from different directions and collided with each other at speed.

My sister was an ambitious girl constantly striving to get ahead. I was not at all competitive by nature and my ambitions were vague and dreamy. I kept up with her despite the natural extra maturity that girls have when growing up and spanned the experience gaps.

Father was a rough diamond. He started off selling sweets before the war. He joined the ARP (the volunteer rescue services) and lost about 12 years of his salaried years as this was a reserved occupation but largely unpaid. When men were killed faster than they could be replaced he was called up at 40. Because of his age he only advanced to sergeant. He was put into combat training as he was the fittest man they could find for the job. Once he was told off for not taking the lead in front of his men who were flagging on a tough assault course. His commanding officer took him to one side and had a quiet word in his ear. "Lawler" he shouted "why are you not leading your men?" "Well sir," he responded, "I can judge their performance best from this position; also by the way this is the only time they will do the course today, I have already done it eleven times and this is my twelfth time". Twelve and time — you see if you bear with me you will see some more patterns in astrology, families and environments that shape peoples lives and careers.

Dad left school at eleven as his mother did not want him to take up his scholarship but to start to earn a living for the family group. After the war my father became a footwear salesman, then a manager and finally a buyer. His boundless physical energy helped him in his commissions with all the major stores and fashion outlets.

During this time he met people from all walks of life and often fitted King Farouk of Saudia Arabia. On some Saturdays I would work in his shop in Fulham fitting the feet of Catholic teaching nuns and their pupils.

Three weeks before he died my father had been repairing the roof. He had a serious illness when young just before starting work, and this last work of his was to herald his demise. He had a weakened chest and lungs from years of trying too hard and he fell ill with a very nasty flu that nearly finished me off as well. I nursed him for three weeks and a retailing friend of his, Eric, who had trained as a doctor syringed his ear two days before he died. Dad was very excited as he could hear a lot better than he had for years. About a month ago Dad had had a minor heart attack and I felt very glum as he went up the ladder, as his brother-in-law Bert had fallen from one a few years before. He would not let me go up and had threatened to go up on his own when I was not in if I did not help him by holding the ladder. The medication given Dad was for bladder and inner ear infections so I was very concerned. Having got him through all this he died fairly peaceably from a congestive heart failure. He may have lived a few months longer if his doctors had given him antibiotics and could have lived a few years with a heart pacemaker. He died while speaking to a ladyfriend on the 'phone. Her son came to investigate but he was too late to help him. Sometimes even seconds count.

One of my uncles came round and went through my father's effects after I had collapsed with grief. The uncle asked about his 'last wishes' (for burial or cremation) while the paramedics and the police did their work. He left with a bulging briefcase, even after being cautioned, leaving me with an empty heart and Kevin the Scottish cop for comfort.

After this all happened my offices were gutted due to a confusion between an architect's plan showing no exits at all, and my business had to be shut down because of dust on my stock and in my lungs. It's all in the sky.

Papers and capers these are the stuff of stars.

Davy O' List (rock and stage star) you get my gist

Will he be famous or his notation never be missed?

Both parents came from families of 11 and 12, so I had about 132 aunts and uncles and many cousins of both sexes. My father would 'adopt' various stray bodies that came into his life through his work and retailing. I had two particular uncles that imposed on me as if I owed them an automatic respect. They would have tried the patience of any saint — one being a chartered accountant who was totally obsessed with political constitutional and legal matters and another that mistook my sensitivity for something else and was always 'trying things on,' often at the point of sundry kitchen knives — a behavioural mode that led me to the waiting rooms of many a child care officer or psychiatrist. On Dad's side was a baker who had been a featherweight boxing champion but he was told he was too light, thin and hence 'unfit' to join the army which separated the men from the boys. When in desperation he was finally called up to replace those stationed away or shot, he grew three and a third inches from age 27 to 33 going from five feet eleven and a half to about six foot three inches. He also put on weight through eating, training and drinking beer, when he came out he had been through all the boxing grades and emerged heavyweight champion. He was 66 when he died; he tripped on a rug and fell over, having survived thousands of blows to the head. He was dispatched to the great boxing ring in the sky by a long wood and metal bar, the fender he fell onto. While stationed in Egypt he often had to go long periods without fluid in the deserts. He made up for this by drinking a barrel of beer at a time, but I would not have described him as a drunk. He was a jovial family man. Seconds out.

My mother was a court dressmaker and worked for Harvey Nichols in Knightsbridge, which catered to the needs of Royalty, often being given the hardest garments to sew, fit and alter. My mother left school at 14 for similar reasons to my father. She died of cancer seven years ahead of him. No one called her dress alterations 'seconds'.

What these genetic forebears say is that my genes held a certain potential. The socialists would say that we fought a war against fascism while ironically I grew up in an environment that intensified the survival of the fittest. My father was not a good speller and often spelt our names wrong on birthday cards but in the end this became part of his folklore and he started to call my sister Margaret a lot of names when she stayed out after eleven with the boys and girls, and Magit or even Maggott as a term of endearment when he felt that she had done well or wanted to win her round to his side against her mother or me.

What my chart says is that I have a certain ease in some circumstances and difficulty in others. We call this a chart potential. Most people do not reach theirs but some holy men manage to transcend their charts. I was strong in my muscles but my weakened heart showed up in the 'Mars in Cancer retrograde' so I could never be a classic Olympic athlete. By training I once flew a man powered flying machine that had been designed and built by colleagues and myself.

Father and Mother had iron stomachs and healthy constitutions. My sister and I both had food sensitivities. My sister had asthma. I had eczema. The astrological links can skip generations much as genes can lie dormant.

With all the aggression and injuries from actions and hostilities ranging from my sister's suitors to hired assassins, I have had to judge situations very quickly. There is nothing more immediate or practical than saving the life of a loved one who is ill or in danger.

While in Amsterdam I wired power of attorney over a fortune in guilders to save the lives of some near relatives. After contacting my brother-in-law I set about their rescue in other ways.

Astrology is a practised art that has a few types of major applications and divisions.

Love compatability (synastry)

Business trends (predictions)

World events (mundane)
Health crises (decumbriture)
Career (natal)
Fun and Profit (electional)
Elections (contest).

I hope that you find this book both an aid to life as well as an entertainment and that the stories can be of some help to you. They are easy to remember, like the stories and parables in the Bible.

In more detail, now you know the point of this here discussion. These points are given to show situations that often arise in astrological consultation. What is the difference between nurture and nature? Does the surrounding sub-culture lead to enlightenment or point people to crime? Can diet overcome innate personality traits to create new abilities?

I had two cousins Peter and Roland who became Olympic canoeists and I got into Westiminster City eight. I was quite good at rowing though I weighed less that our guiding cox in the boat. I did not inherit their mechanical skills with cars and motorbikes although I have patented the odd invention and given medical research findings to the public domain of international world health.

In summary, in life we have complex problems that require fine judgement. Often one has to weigh conflicting views or indicators. All personality traits are not active at the same time. Circumstances and contexts change events; there is a natural rough justice that operates as well.

To illustrate the scope of chart analysis I have given factual accounts of events as we can be more objective about these although even here there is no absolute truth.

Emotional liaisons and feelings are the stock in trade of the astrologer and although prediction is an issue the main purpose of having your map monitored is to help you reach your full potential in life.

As an astrologer I have had to give advice to 3 kings, ministers of church and state and a Queen mother. My father and mother had contacts with royalty through the work they did. There are similarities and differences. The chart, wheel or horoscope helps you decide about life, people and events. A bad workman will blame his tools. Astrology gives us excellent tools; it is up to us to learn to apply and develop our skills. One may be able to turn a vicious person towards the light but I do not feel compelled to preach, proselytise or disseminate.

My faith tells me that whoever steals or does wrong will be punished. Thy will be done on earth as it is in heaven. As above so below.

Astrology does not compel. If there is a waltz playing the best options are to dance along or sit it out. There is no physical force preventing us from doing a tango, but there is a tide that taken at the flood allows us to surf-ride to fortune!

Thus in my short life I have been a research chemist and worked on brain chemistry (Parkinsonism) at Philips Duphar in Weesp and drug side reactions through study of breakdown products. I have been a professional dancer in the Buddha ballets in Paris, Covent Garden and Hong Kong.

Three times I have worked at the Stock Exchange when there have been new ideas and financial crises. Charm,

Bargain Accounting, Talisman, Big Bang, Gems, Oscar, Torus. You can forecast financial trends with astrology too.

I have given time money and goods to charities and have been financial director of the Simplified Spelling Society while Prince (Phil the Greek) Philip was patron.

Films I have been involved with include cartoons on cluster analysis for saving lives through accident and insurance safeguards, parapsychology documentaries and the feature film 'Legend of the Witches' where I played the new initiate, doing the many lifethreatening stunts myself. This film toured the West End of London for six years as a major hit.

I have been on TV as an alternative healer and graphologist (handwriting analyst) speaking about the sports writer Paul Johnston.

Like the stories, this account can be read again and you will see the patterns emerge like growing children.

Still there is more to come.

The horoscope shows the way.